The Adventure of the Colonial Boy

By

Narrelle M Harris

Paperback ISBN 978-0-9935136-2-6
ePub ISBN 978-0-9935136-3-3

Published in the UK by Improbable Press Limited
71-75 Shelton Street, Covent Garden, London, WC2H 9JQ
Cover design by www.staunch.com

For

Verity and Br0-Harry,
for all the love you gave us in words and art,
and all you have for each other.

Chapter One

Doctor John Watson found no relief from grief when he placed the final manuscripts for *The Strand Magazine* into an envelope. No; this memorial in text to his dead friend rendered the wound raw again, as though he was the one who'd done the murder at Reichenbach Falls, rather than that villain Moriarty. To write that sorry tale had made it true, dashing the last of Watson's denial.

Sherlock Holmes was dead, murdered by his great enemy and failed by his great friend.

Watson sealed the envelope, contemplating its contents gravely. For all the things he'd altered in his stories – to protect the innocent, to make a better tale, to obscure truths he was hardly able to articulate – one incident had been utterly unfabricated.

On learning Moriarty had escaped their net, Holmes had urged Watson to return to England, saying, 'You'll find me a dangerous companion now.' Watson's reply had been unequivocal. 'I will not go, Holmes. Nothing you say will induce me to leave your side in this business.'

Except that Holmes had induced him away, after all. He'd done it slyly, casually. The memory of it filled Watson with a hot flash of anger, and afterwards with guilt.

I'm angry with myself, not Holmes.

Watson didn't doubt Holmes had done it with the best of intentions; but Watson had returned to their Swiss boarding house at Holmes's greatest hour of need. For that, he could not forgive himself. After all those years working together, of their

4

close friendship, he should have divined that the message about the sick Englishwoman was false.

Holmes's deliberate choice to let Watson leave did not, to Watson's mind, lessen his failure to stay by Holmes's side: not with the consequences that his failure entailed.

Well, the final story was written now. *The Strand Magazine* would publish Watson's remaining tales, however fancifully embellished. Each sprang from a true event and it would be for the public to read, judging both Holmes's genius and Watson's own fault in the matter.

Watson checked his pocket watch; it was not yet midday. A walk would do him good after so many days cloistered in his rooms, writing and rewriting.

He rose and pulled his dark coat over his black suit. He smoothed the black ribbon around the crown of his hat, put it on, then the black gloves.

Envelope tucked under one arm, he took his walking stick in hand and set out to deliver the manuscripts to *The Strand's* offices in Burleigh Street.

Afterwards, he would visit the cemetery and tell Mary that, for good or ill, the work was done at last.

The walk to South Kensington Station was pleasant on this clear September day. Watson stood on the platform, awaiting the train to Embankment, and watched its counterpart draw in on the other platform: the train to Baker Street. Watson's mouth pursed as the train departed, tugging him in the direction of those old rooms: of happier memories and the life he missed.

A sudden crowd of people jostled the doctor towards the platform's edge as his train drew in. Watson clutched tight to his manuscripts – he'd be damned if he lost the things by spilling them on the tracks – and braced against the unruly bustling. Someone behind him cursed, another man growled a response, and a hard shove shot Watson towards the lip of the platform. Only by jamming the tip of his cane into the ground was he saved from being propelled in front of the groaning, steaming bulk of the engine.

Watson turned angrily but the thoughtless instigators of his near miss had vanished. Scowling, he entered the train car and braced against the jerk and sway as it rolled into motion.

Alighting at Embankment he made his way up into the fresh air, strolling through the Victoria Gardens alongside the Thames, down the lane behind the Savoy, then up the short flight of stairs to The Strand.

There, he paused, arrested by memories prompted by those familiar buildings; the clop of hooves and rattle of carriages; the voices of men hailing one another or a hansom; the dust and smell of it, with the blue sky overhead, all the bustle and life of the London metropolis caught in microcosm.

This had been their London. The London of Holmes and Watson. How often had their adventures brought them here? What strange tales and astonishing mysteries had led them like hounds through these streets and alleys, into dingy boarding houses and smoky dens, or into handsomely furnished offices, grand halls, homes with a history of great or faded fortunes?

All of those wondrous exploits and their dazzling conclusions were at an end now. London was less than she had been, diminished by the loss of Sherlock Holmes, as was Watson.

The stories he'd written in a near frenzy over the last few years washed colour over the whole once more, painting every part of the city with the memory of the great detective. But nothing could truly capture the sound of Holmes's voice ringing out with thrilling purpose, the rich delight of his laughter, or the way they had laughed at absurdities. No words on paper could truly describe the bright gleam in Holmes's eye as he latched onto the clue that spelled doom for some malefactor; or the warm flush of Holmes's cheeks as his lassitude was galvanised into decisive activity. Nor the elegance of Holmes's hands, his gait, his whole person, whether engaged in a case or playing his violin to soothe Watson's fractured nerves…

Distracted by melancholy, Watson began to cross the great thoroughfare for Burleigh Street when a shout warned him of a carriage bearing down on him. Clutching the envelope and stepping aside, he found the horse had altered course and still bore down on him.

The driver had his fist tight-wrapped around the whip, which he brought down hard. The beast, eyes rolling against its hard use, lurched faster and would have run him down, except that a hand on Watson's collar jerked him back onto the footpath.

'Doctor Watson!' cried his rescuer, 'Watch your step! That growler almost had you, and then what would our old friend Mr Holmes have said to me, hmm? He wouldn't have been happy, I'll tell you that for free.'

Watson, frowning after the disappearing carriage, turned at the familiar voice. 'Why, Wiggins, is that you? I hardly recognise you!'

'To the life,' beamed Wiggins. He was much changed from the grubby street urchin who had been such an important part of life at Baker Street. He was a young man now, with the side-whiskers to prove it.

'Didn't Holmes find work for you as a messenger for *The Graphic*?'

'He did, and made sure I learned my letters and all. The editor liked my way with words, he said, and my colourful observations upon the life and denizens of the lower-down byways of London. He's training me up to be a reporter, now.'

Watson peered at the young man's hands and clothes. 'And you begin by drawing sketches of those denizens, I see.'

Wiggins laughed. 'You see the sketchbook in one coat pocket and my pencils in the other, Doctor Watson!'

'And the smudges upon your wrist, hand and fingers,' agreed Watson, 'The deduction was, as our friend would have said, elementary.'

'He'd no doubt have told you a dozen more things besides,' said Wiggins.

'Indeed, he would.'

'Such as I'm stepping out with Gill the Baker's daughter, Jane, who's a peach, though her father don't approve of me.' Wiggins's merry countenance sobered at last, his gaze flickering between the black band on Watson's hat and his black cotton gloves. 'I heard about your missus, Doctor Watson. I was very sorry for it, too. Mrs Watson was always very kind to me and the boys, if she happened on us, and she made that dolly for Georgie's sister Lottie when she was sick and we came to you.'

'Mary was a good soul,' said Watson, then ceased to speak, for what else could he say?

Wiggins recognised that here was a well of loss much too deep for easy conversation.

'Well, Doctor, I must be off to finish my drawings for Mr Rowley. You looked to be in a hurry yourself, taking more of your splendid stories to *The Strand Magazine*, I've no doubt. It's been grand to read them, and remember the great things Mr Holmes did. Even if I detect a little of what Mr Rowley calls artistic licence in them from time to time. Storytelling isn't courtroom testimony, is it Doctor Watson? No more than news is, says my editor.'

'No doubt your editor is right. Holmes was fond of *The Graphic* for its personal advertisements and a gossip column that assisted on more than one occasion.'

'I'll tell Mr Rowley so. He'll be right proud, what with your stories making Mr Holmes such a popular man about the country these days. Well, I hope to see you again, Doctor.'

'And I, you,' said Watson, 'And thank you for your timely intervention. Today has been a day for rowdy travellers, I'm afraid.'

Wiggins raised a hand in farewell and then was off, whistling, to find some local life to sketch for his paper. Watson gripped his walking stick and, with no further incidents, took his parcel of stories to the magazine's offices.

Some twenty minutes later, Watson was again out in the London early autumn, having irritably declined tea with his editor after their final exchange.

'Are you sure you won't reconsider, Doctor Watson? Holmes's exploits are so very popular with the reading public; I could publish them weekly for years to come.'

'Would that I could oblige you,' Watson had replied, jaw aching from gritting his teeth, 'But as Holmes died in Switzerland two and a half years ago, as I told you, I'm afraid there is no more suitable material for me to draw upon.'

'Surely you could invent…?' began the editor, then fell silent, no doubt quelled by the spark of rage he'd ignited in Watson's countenance. 'No, of course not. I see that. It's only that he is such a great loss to the field of criminology. To London, too. Our readers do quite feel that they know him, you know.'

'I'm pleased to hear it,' said Watson. That had been in part his intention: that the world should truly know his friend and understand the great loss he and they had suffered with his passing, 'But the fact remains there is nothing more to tell. He died defending them from a cruel and subtle mastermind of crime, and they should know it.'

'Indeed.' The editor had smiled. 'He was a hero, after Thomas Carlyle's notions, or so you write him.'

'And so he was,' said Watson stiffly, offended, 'At least to the degree that any flawed yet gifted human being may choose to behave as one.'

'I've no doubt of it,' the editor replied, backpedalling from any insinuation of exaggeration.

Watson had said his farewells and left in a simmering temper.

Certainly the stories were exaggerated in parts, but never Holmes's brilliance in solving the crimes. If sometimes he shone more light on Holmes's genius than his own contribution, what of that? Demonstrating Holmes's singular mind and great achievements had been the *point* of the stories. Where Watson had known things that Holmes had already understood, and it made better narrative sense to delay the reveal, why of *course* that's what he'd done. As in his telling of the tragic affair he'd written up as the Boscombe Valley case: Watson had known the Ballarat connection from the start, having spent formative years in the colony of Victoria. He'd in no way exaggerated Holmes's prowess; only written the tale to display it to best advantage.

And Holmes had certainly not been perfect. His surliness during Watson's courtship and marriage was a case in point, although he seemed to think well enough of Mary. Given time, he'd even deigned to visit them occasionally. But Holmes had let it be known since the moment she'd crossed their threshold – and Watson had dared to indicate that he thought her lovely – that love and marriage were the grossest sentimental claptrap and utterly anathema to him. He'd been downright waspish on the subject, which had merely served to convince Watson that he was correct to pursue Mary. Clearly there was no further profit in hoping...even had the strictures of society not prevented them from...

Watson's mind shied from completing either thought. Instead, he walked briskly, preferring the distracting bustle and energy of the task over a hansom or the Underground. He was alone with his thoughts too much already. A walk provided plenty of London's daily hubbub to keep his mind far from such dangerous and futile avenues.

At the cemetery, Watson bought a posy of violets from a dishevelled little girl at the gate. A grander bunch of flowers might be more appropriate, but Mary had always bought posies from the women and girls near their home, delighting in the simple blooms of violets, bluebells or heliotropes – and in the simple help such purchases offered to the poorer women of their town. So Watson bought flowers from little street urchins because Mary would have liked that.

At Mary's plot, he knelt to clear away the last visit's flowers and place the new posy in its decorative pot. A simple wooden marker bearing the name *Mary Watson* stood at the head of the grave. The soil had not yet properly settled; the gravestone itself wouldn't be placed for another few months.

'Here you are, my dear,' said Watson gently, 'Violets. I'll bring heliotropes next time. I remember they were your favourite.'

He shifted to give his leg room to stretch – the damned thing still twinged after hard use, and the incident at the Underground station had jarred it. He massaged his aching knee, thinking grumpily of all the wags who had written to tell him where he did and did not have a wound. Some seemed to think that being shot once somehow excluded being shot twice in that terrible killing field.

Watson dug his thumb into the old scar and felt the tight muscle loosen at last. He shifted his position so that the knee wouldn't cramp again. Once settled, he took off his mourning gloves and laid a bare hand over the grave, almost as though he still held Mary's hand in his.

'Well, Mary, it's done. I've written every story that I could about him. I can't say that it's given me peace yet, but perhaps that will come. I'm sorry you couldn't be here for the end, but thank you for being the start of it. It's almost been like being with him again, to write them. And you were right. They serve as a monument to him, since he can't have a grave.'

No body had ever been found, and so Holmes had no burial place. Even Moriarty had washed ashore at a little village days later, but of Holmes there'd been nothing but a bedraggled scarf.

The lack of Holmes's body (Watson could never think the word *corpse*) made the almost unbearable news very difficult to accept, despite the fact that Watson had seen the killing ground and all the evidence – including Holmes's treasured note – for himself.

The lack was worse even than a burial at sea, Holmes's body cast adrift with no plot of soil, no memorial. It gave a sense of unreality to Watson's loss, and gave his grief no anchor where it could come at last to rest.

His Mary had understood how his grief had cast him adrift. She had suggested he take up his pen again, to make a monument to his dear friend in words if there could not be one of stone.

And so Watson set about writing one. All of the stories, including that awful, final story, would be published each month until the end of this year. The world would finally know what a champion it had lost.

'I miss you both terribly,' Watson said softly, flexing his fingers in the green grass. 'My two great friends.'

He and Mary had been very fond of each other, even if theirs had never been a towering passion.

On the first anniversary of Holmes's death, Watson had returned home drunk, weeping and apologising for not being the husband she deserved.

'Hush, John,' Mary had soothed him, 'You're a good husband. You're kind and gentle and generous. I know we're more friends than lovers, but I'm content. I'm mistress of my own household here, and not a servant in another's. You allow me so much independence, and to run the business of the practice, which I know you hate. It bores you so. I know how much you miss him.'

'You are the very best of women,' he'd told her. *But he was the best part of my life.*

He often wondered if he'd spoken the latter out loud to her. If so, she'd never admonished him with it. Next day, when he'd recovered, they never spoke of it. He never drank to excess again while she was alive. He couldn't trust himself.

Watson brushed his moustache with his knuckles, to cover the tight pursing of his lips and hide the sudden surge of emotion.

Watson would have mourned Sherlock Holmes as fully and as long as the dear Queen still mourned her consort, but they had been friends, no more. It was unseemly for his grief to be expressed for more than a month. It was unseemly to be so mired in grief at all, and for someone not his wife. For a *man*, no less. So Watson had worn his dark suit and armband for the month and packed his sorrow away inside himself afterwards. Mary knew, of course – hence her suggestion that he write.

She felt – they both did – that if he could write these stories, Watson could at last let go of his grief. He could let go of Holmes and resume a full life with Mary.

Watson patted the soil under his fingertips. Oh, his good and sweet-natured Mary. Had any man ever been so fortunate in his choice of bride? She'd ever been kind about his attachment to Holmes, never grudging the time he spent chasing *outré* mysteries of the type that had brought her to their door.

Far from pining at home, Mary had taken up the running of the household and the practice, as though born to manage such affairs. After Switzerland, Watson, never terribly interested in the business side of his practice – and frankly barely interested in the medical side of it, given his years as an army doctor and then at Holmes's side – continued to leave those matters in his wife's capable hands.

Mary had been patient but ever forward-looking. They tried again and again for a child. Each of the miscarriages was devastating.

The last miscarriage, three months ago, had been the most devastating of all. All his medical knowledge and skill had proven useless, just as all his courage and strength had been useless when Holmes had met his end. Their daughter was birthed dead, the cord around her little neck. Mary had bled and bled and bled from the arduous labour and fruitless delivery, and nothing could be done. Mother and daughter died hours apart. Their new beginning had become instead an echo of a bloody battlefield death.

Here in the churchyard, by the grave in which his wife and daughter lay, a grieving thought came to him.

I'm a widower twice over.

The unbidden thought startled him. The words were new, but the feeling was not. Twice bereft, and the account of Holmes's death he had lately written had entwined that loss along with Mary's now.

I'm a widower twice over. Childless, wifeless, friendless.

Watson grimaced. He brushed the loamy soil from his fingers and proceeded to pull the more vulgar growths from the site: dandelions, a tuft of knapweed and a single sprouting thistle.

'I'm not sure what I'll do with myself now,' Watson told the grave as he pulled out the unwanted plants, 'The thought of continuing in general practice appals me. I have much more sympathy now for Holmes's perpetual cry of tedium. Perhaps I should follow Wiggins' lead and try my hand at journalism, though I hear there may be an opportunity to work as a police surgeon. I'm not so sure Scotland Yard will have me. Every corporal, sergeant and detective there thinks Lestrade, Gregson and Jones are based on them. Of course, some of them are right, but I challenge them to accurately identify themselves. Half of them think they inspired Bradstreet, and he's actually real. '

Watson pushed the little vase of flowers more firmly into the earth, taking pleasure in the simple comforts of the scent of soil, violets and other greenery, of bees humming in the flowering rose shrub along a nearby plot while birds called overhead, and of the warm sun on his skin that reminded him of hard yet happy days toiling on his father's gold claim before the scandal struck.

Had he not been so attuned to nature in that moment, Watson might have missed the subtle hiss that sent the hair standing on end up his arms and neck to every follicle in his scalp.

Then he saw it – the sinuous coils of an adder writhing towards him over Mary's grave, dark grey scales marked with a black zig-zag stripe, red eyes unblinking as it slithered towards his bare hand. The reptile – the only venomous snake native to these isles – compacted its great coils as its mouth opened, revealing glistening fangs, and rose up, about to strike.

Watson, too, reared back, snatching up his walking stick as the creature struck and missed. The heavy weight of its body barely fell as it curled and coiled about for a second attack. Watson swung his cane like a cricket bat at the lunging narrow head. If those fangs once connected with his skin, he'd be in for an ugly death.

The thought both chilled him and steeled his resolve.

The stick connected hard with the creature, but Watson was too experienced to be complacent. He swung the cane down and beat the venomous thing on the head once, twice, then a third time to be sure. It lay twitching gruesomely until he took up a stone from the path and beat its head until it was of no further danger.

Watson stood, one fist clasped around the bloodied stone, the other around his cane, his breath coming fast yet steady, his eyes bright, skin flushed. He was surprised to realise he was smiling. Oh, but that reminded him of the old days of adventure! Even though the matter was nothing more sinister than an adder disturbed while sunbaking. He felt more alive, more awake, than he had in years. *Since Switzerland.*

His smile faded. Mary had been his friend, a good wife and business partner, and he had loved her in that fashion. But she'd never been the one to light the fire in his breast.

He is dead and she is dead and I deserved neither and I'm alone. Again.

Watson flung the lifeless snake and the stone into the shrub, wiped his hand on his handkerchief and left the cemetery, as melancholy as when he had arrived.

He was wholly unprepared for the telegram awaiting him in his lonely Kensington home.

It lay with the early mail on the sideboard. At first, Watson let it be. He wished to wash his hands after so strenuous and sorrowful a morning. A peculiar morning, as well. Providence had clearly chosen to present him, preoccupied as he was with Holmes, with grotesqueries as strange as those that once heralded a tangled and dangerous case.

With clean hands, Watson took up the mail and in the spirit of his strange day, decided to employ Holmes's methods in sorting it. That thin, cheap envelope no doubt harboured a request for donations to worthy causes that Mary had supported. Next was a sturdier envelope, address typewritten, which smacked strongly of a bill that he was in no mood to see. He set these aside and regarded the telegram and the final, thick envelope with a frown.

He ought to open the telegram, but he couldn't imagine it contained good news. Gone were the days when such missives were the harbingers of great adventures.

The envelope was of thick, high quality paper, also typewritten but unlike any official letter he'd ever received from a creditor or a bank. A friend or acquaintance would surely have handwritten the address. In any case, Watson couldn't think of a single acquaintance who'd use such excellent paper.

It might have been mail related to the *Strand* stories, but those often pedantic missives generally went either to Burleigh Street, or to Baker Street. Mrs Hudson sent them to him every week or so through one of the street boys.

The letter was one more mystery in a day of oddities.

Well, if a mystery was to be combined with bad news, he'd like at least to have some strong drink as recompense.

Watson poured a measure of scotch from the decanter, took up the letter opener, and slit open the telegram.

He stared at it for long moments before it fell from his trembling fingers onto the desk.

It read:

Come at once if convenient. If inconvenient, come all the same. – S.H.

Chapter Two

Doctor Watson stared at the telegram, his mouth dry, his heart racing. The initial shock – a surge of joy shrivelling to cinders at the almost instant realisation that it couldn't possibly be from Holmes – gave way to the most incandescent blaze of utter rage.

The first telegram Holmes had sent Watson to summon him from his cosy hearth at his and Mary's new home had read thus. Watson had immediately risen to his feet, startling Mary with his urgency. Once she'd seen the summons, she'd smiled and said that of course he must go.

It became a private joke, that Holmes would send for him with that wording: *Come at once if convenient. If inconvenient, come all the same. – S.H.* Those words had augured so many exciting and happy times, in cases both wonderful and dreadful.

Watson hadn't written of those telegrams in any of his stories, not even the ones today delivered to the publisher. This little joke he and Holmes had shared was too personal to place in print.

And now someone had dared play such a cruel and hurtful trick as to send him a telegram, as though from Holmes, to summon him to God only knew where. Watson had half a mind to find out so that he could go along and thrash the fellow. Instead, he screwed up the yellow paper and pitched it into the wastebasket by his desk.

Refusing to think more about it, Watson attacked the mysterious letter with the silver-bladed opener. Within were a number of folded, official-looking papers. More puzzled than ever, he drew out the bundle and flattened each upon the desk.

The doctor's quizzical frown deepened. On opening the documents, he found a ticket on the steamship *Lenora Ann*, in the name of Doctor Ormond Sacker. On closer inspection, the ticket proved to be for a first class berth. The destination: Melbourne, in the colony of Victoria.

Behind this ticket was a letter of introduction, which begged Captain Esmond Deville of the *Lenora Ann* to provide all aid to Doctor Sacker on his journey and disembarkation. A second letter was addressed to one Mrs Gallagher, proprietress of a guest house on Collins Street in Melbourne, recommending Doctor Sacker as a tenant.

Watson turned the envelope over in his hand, sure that he had read it correctly, and there, yes!, was his own name and address, typewritten upon the outside. Yet all of its contents related to travel documents for this Doctor Sacker.

An immediate suspicion unfurled in Watson's mind. It expanded with several other equally unpalatable surmises. Teeth gritted in anger, Watson retrieved the crumpled telegram from the wastebasket and smoothed it out upon the desk.

The telegram had been sent to him from Palmerston, a port on the north coast of Australia. Hadn't Darwin on his *Beagle* seen the harbour there? Watson recalled a reported gold strike near the town, the year before he'd enrolled in medical school. He'd wondered at the time whether his father had gone there to try his terrible luck once more.

Memory of his father and therefore of his late brother made Watson scowl and soured his temper further.

Some damned charlatan intended to lure him to the other side of the world by pretending to be Holmes, unaware that Holmes was dead.

Or, said the writerly part of his mind, the over-imaginative part that longed for Holmes's death to be recognised as a terrible mistake, surely to be rectified – *or it is Holmes himself, alive, by god.* Alive!

The lurch of desperate hope plummeted as swiftly once more into fury. Watson honestly didn't know which prospect made him the more livid. Either instance was a cruel trick, the one perpetrated by some old enemy or new antagonist filled with spite, and the other, *oh,* the other, perpetrated by his dearest friend, the man he...

Watson bundled up the papers and shoved them haphazardly into his pocket, before drawing on his coat, hat and gloves and storming out of the house, hardly knowing what he'd say when he reached his destination.

His arrived at Baker Street, keeping his temper with some effort so as not to alarm Mrs Hudson or rouse her own rare but intimidating temper. He had first truly witnessed her ire after she'd realised that his stories represented her as a woman much older than her actual years – in her late thirties, when he and Holmes had first resided at Baker Street. 'To protect your privacy,' he'd protested at her sharp irritation.

'You might have named me Mrs Smith, then, and not given the address!'

But that had been in the first book, when Watson had thought to encourage business to their door. Mrs Hudson had forgiven him, eventually, and only because she was entertained by having such venturesome lodgers.

After necessary greetings, however, Watson ran out of patience for niceties.

'You haven't received any letters or parcels of any kind?' he asked, 'You've not been bothered by strangers asking after me?'

'Oh, plenty of those, Doctor Watson,' said Mrs Hudson, her mild Scottish burr intensifying with wry amusement, 'Hardly a day goes by without some impertinent fellow or other wanting to see Mr Holmes or yourself. Some refuse to believe that it's impossible. Last week, one even made it all the way into the house, intruded upon the rooms and began to go through Mr Holmes's papers! I had to chase him out with a broom!' Her tone was filled with hearty satisfaction.

'Last week?' Watson asked, puzzled, 'But surely 221B does not still contain Holmes's papers.'

'His papers, his pipes, his scientific equipment, his clothes, his music and violin: all of it!'

'But why hasn't his brother come to clear it all away?'

Mrs Hudson's expression softened into kindness. 'Mr Mycroft Holmes says he can't bring himself to do so. He pays the rent and begs that I leave everything as it is until he has the heart for it. It is, I suppose, an easier tenancy to have papers but no Mr Holmes to make his terrible messes, though I confess I miss him. As I know you do.' Mrs Hudson patted Watson's arm. 'It's much too quiet without you both. Even on his own he was too quiet by half. I believe he was lonely, once you married, though he pretended otherwise.'

Oblivious to Watson's troubled reaction to this claim, Mrs Hudson patted his arm again. 'I suppose you must be lonely yourself, now, Doctor. The service for Mrs Watson was very lovely, though, and you spoke so beautifully. If you'd ever like a landlady once more, I'd be so glad to have you back, when Mr Holmes's brother feels he can manage to clear the rooms.'

Watson avoided giving an answer, not knowing how to reconcile the sudden longing to come back to Baker Street with the anguish at the thought of returning alone to the home where he and Holmes had nurtured their friendship.

'I must see Mycroft Holmes.' If Mrs Hudson had no clues for him, then surely the brother, whom Holmes had declared had "art in the blood" to an even greater degree than himself, might.

Watson thought it ominous that Mycroft Holmes maintained his brother's rooms. He wouldn't have believed either of the Holmeses to be so sentimental. *Ominous or auspicious.* As with many things touching on this shocking matter, he was not sure how to feel. So much depended on the truth behind these bizarre communications.

He made his way in rising agitation to Whitehall and thence to the inconspicuous entrance of the well-appointed but discreet Diogenes Club, close to Queen Anne's Gate. He'd been here once before, to deliver the terrible news of Holmes's loss to his only known relative. At the time Mycroft had seemed unruffled, though kind enough towards Watson's own barely-contained grief.

Too much didn't make sense.

He managed at least to hold his tongue on reaching the Diogenes and being shown into the Strangers' Room, where he pulled off his gloves and hat, thumped them onto the table. He proceeded to march up and down, his stride as martial as if he were off to war.

Mycroft Holmes's bulk filled the doorway. The door itself was not yet closed before Watson bent a blazing eye on him.

'Tell me straight, Mr Holmes. Why do I hear from Mrs Hudson that you're maintaining Holmes's flat?'

Mycroft Holmes did not betray alarm at the sudden exclamation. Instead, he ignored Watson for as long as it took to pour the doctor and himself each a glass of brandy from the cabinet.

'You are much exercised, Doctor Watson.'

'I have had a vexing morning, and it grows more puzzling. I went to Mrs Hudson seeking news on whether some scoundrel had used her to send me a most insolent communication. She told me you are keeping our old rooms intact and untenanted.'

Mycroft Holmes's sad smile halted Watson in his indignation.

'It is so,' said Mycroft Holmes, 'And no-one is more surprised than I, that I find the finalisation of my brother's affairs so difficult. I'm sure that Sherlock would blame it on what he calls my infernal laziness, but the truth is that it's a sad business. He was my last living close relative, and each time I feel that I should tend to the matter, I find that my feet will take me anywhere but Baker Street.'

Watson knew that heartsore condition only too well. He had been to Baker Street but a handful of times since Holmes's death, and only when he had a purpose that couldn't be avoided.

With less violence than he'd initially intended, Watson took the papers from his pocket and presented them to the elder Holmes.

'I received these papers this morning,' he said, allowing Mycroft Holmes to take them from his fingers, 'This telegram uses the very wording with which Holmes once called me to cases at Baker Street. What intolerable scheme is this? Who would find profit in such cruel humour?'

Mycroft perused the papers, one eyebrow raised. 'These are indeed curious and, as you say, unkind. Who do you believe sent them to you?'

'I could not possibly guess.' Watson's mouth and brow were drawn into tight, unhappy lines, for his heart was too troubled and his mind too confused to express the deduction that hovered at the fringe of thought. *Your brother is alive and has sent for me.* The notion was too mad and too cruel for utterance.

The words dried in his mouth, moreover, at the searching look to which Mycroft Holmes subjected him. He had once been used to such looks from Sherlock Holmes, as Holmes examined and calculated and deduced Watson's day from signs and marks upon his skin and clothes, his known habits and principles.

'I observe that you have had a remarkable and unhappy day, Doctor Watson,' said Mycroft.

Watson grit his teeth. When Holmes had played this game with him, there had been a great deal of humour and warmth in the exercise. The same scrutiny from Mycroft Holmes felt much more intrusive. 'I told you as much when I arrived.'

'So you did. You made a final delivery of those most entertaining fictions to *The Strand Magazine,* I perceive, and paid a visit to your late wife's grave, where you had a most dangerous encounter, but not the sole one of the day. There have been multiple attempts on your life this morning, Doctor.'

26

'Nonsense,' snapped Watson, 'Only some near misses with unruly traffic and a chance encounter with an adder.'

Mycroft Holmes raised an eyebrow. Watson huffed out a breath designed to anchor him as he unconsciously stood to attention. 'It was, as you say, a very strange day. I returned home to this telegram and that parcel of documents. What am I to make of it, then?'

Mycroft Holmes, not to be rushed, turned the papers over and over in his hand. He even sniffed the thick envelope full of tickets. Watson, aware of how Holmes had once poured over clues in the same manner, couldn't help thinking this was a pantomime of sorts. 'What's the meaning of it?' he demanded impatiently, his voice less commanding and more rough with emotion than he'd intended.

'Calm yourself, Doctor.'

Watson stood quivering with indignation before the portly Holmes. 'How can I be calm? I must know the purpose of this hideous practical joke.'

'But is it a joke, Doctor Watson?'

'It must be. It cannot be from your brother.' *Surely he would not have treated me in this cavalier manner.*

Mycroft Holmes pulled on his lower lip. 'That is unlikely. However, this name,' he tapped a thick forefinger on the name Ormond Sacker, 'Has very particular antecedents. Pray, take a seat, Doctor Watson. I may be able to enlighten you to some degree, although much remains unclear.'

Watson sat as directed. He took a bracing gulp of the brandy to settle his nerves. Much restored, he sat, alert, waiting for Mycroft Holmes to elucidate matters.

'First of all, I understand you know more of Moriarty and his previous clashes with Sherlock than you have written of. Certainly more than you have ever discussed, except with my brother.'

'Not even with Mary,' Watson assured him, 'At Holmes's urging, to protect her and a number of our clients and cases trammelled up with his schemes. I've recorded their final encounter and its conclusion, as you know, and delivered it today to *The Strand Magazine*. Beyond that, I have kept silent, as he wished.'

'Sherlock was aware that certain of the Professor's schemes touched upon matters of state. Your manuscript, which you were kind enough to send me, demonstrates that you're aware that in the final action, a number of Moriarty's lieutenants also escaped the net. Her Majesty's finest agents have been operating in the field in the years since Moriarty and my brother's death to stem the last of that tide of crime and treachery. This name here, Ormond Sacker, was an alias last used by one such agent, with whom we lost contact in spring this year, when he was in the Colony of Natal. The reappearance of the Sacker name may infer that the agent was not killed after all, or it may indicate that some other fate befell him and that either a fellow agent or, less likely, an enemy, is using it to enlist your assistance in the ongoing assignments.'

'But why communicate with me, and in this fashion? And why now?'

'The timing may well be coincidental, though I hardly think so, with three separate attempts made on your life this day alone.'

Watson's swallowed the last of the brandy, though in his agitation he spilled a little over his fingers. He mopped up the liquor with his handkerchief – remembering suddenly how he'd employed another earlier to clean his hands from the adder's blood – and he looked beseechingly at Mycroft Holmes.

'Has someone truly been attempting to kill me?'

'So I read it, Doctor Watson. It beggars belief to accept that three close accidents on the day you receive this telegram and the accompanying parcel are unrelated. As to your first question – well, Sherlock's reports to the Government showed that you knew almost as much as he on these cases. Certainly you retain your notes. Perhaps your advice and assistance are vital. If the trail has taken our agent to one of our Australian colonies, where I believe you lived for a time, it must be important.'

'Indeed. If any of Moriarty's black crew remains free, then I'd certainly be prepared to do my utmost to see the end of them. We fought too hard and lost too much to allow these lawbreakers to continue with their criminal activities.'

'It relieves me to hear you say so, Doctor Watson, for I believe you must depart, using these tickets, without delay. I would very much appreciate it if you'd investigate the matter. It may be dangerous, of course. I surmise that Her Majesty's own agent has sent the summons, but I can't be certain. It may be a trap.'

'And it may be a genuine appeal for assistance,' said Watson staunchly.

'Indeed. And the risks of ignoring a true appeal may outweigh the risks of subterfuge. You would at least be forearmed with caution. What do you say, Doctor – will you act on Her Majesty's behalf to help her agent complete my brother's work?'

'I should be glad to render any service I may to Her Majesty.'

'Good man. I shall send a porter to your home to pack for you. You may lodge in my spare room in Pall Mall until the *Lenora Ann* sets sail on Friday, which is the day after tomorrow.'

'Surely not,' said Watson, thunderstruck, 'You can't mean that I leave London at a moment's notice for the Antipodes? And who is to say that a final attempt on my life – if indeed those incidents today have been assassination attempts – won't be made on the voyage?'

'I believe that to be most unlikely. If you fail to return to your rooms at all today, they can't pick up your trail, except through the Diogenes Club, and as you well know, this is not a club of talkative men.' Mycroft Holmes beamed, pleased with his little joke about his notorious club where speech even among members was forbidden.

'What of my practice? My *luggage*?'

'The luggage and necessities of travel can easily be obtained, if you'll give me your latchkey. As for your practice – it's easy to see you have been unhappy with the work. If you're amenable, I know of a man seeking a medical practice in your very neighbourhood. If you would allow me to handle so delicate a transaction, I'll see to it that you get a fair price.'

The more cautious part of Doctor Watson knew this to be precipitous and potentially ill-advised. Who was it who summoned him, and so callously with Sherlock Holmes's own words? What ill-famed lieutenant of Moriarty's had slipped the net and was even now conspiring to murder him, to keep him from answering the summons? What contribution had he to make to such a manhunt?

Yet he was heartsore. Now the stories were written, a chasm of lonely days and nights, of listlessness and boredom, opened before him. Grief was still his daily companion. Here instead was the offer of, at the very least, distraction.

He'd sworn never to return to Australia, but he'd been a boy then, flying from scandal and disaster. Now he was middle-aged and once more cut off from family and friend alike. And after all – why not? Whatever the assignment held, whatever the challenges, anything would be better than this slow wasting away from sorrow here in London.

Watson's blood stirred at the old call to action. He would answer it, travel back to the land that had taken so much from him, and if he came upon any confederate of Moriarty's, well then, he'd at last have his vengeance on that gang for murdering his friend.

He might also have a crisp word in season for the agent who had sent him that telegram, too, not least to discover how he'd known of the long-standing and private joke. Watson's anger still simmered from the shock he'd received on opening the telegram. The impersonation of his friend remained a cruel and unnecessary ploy. He'd certainly make his feelings on the subject known.

The deeper and more complicated disappointment – that the message was not from Holmes after all – he would keep to himself.

'I'll do it,' said Doctor Watson firmly, shaking Mycroft Holmes's hand with a steady grip.

Chapter Three

Upon disembarking at Palmerston in the north of Australia early in the month of September, Sherlock Holmes stowed his meagre luggage at an insalubrious hostel for sailors before resuming the hunt. He found his quarry among the drinkers and opium smokers at an even dingier establishment. His enemy was befriending a Chinese miner from the gold diggings. The discussion was of a young fellow Chinaman who had in recent days sought information about passage south.

Holmes lost them in the unlit streets, however, and had to retire for the night. He still limped, though the knife wound was mending well. He had little patience for the injury. It was his own fault for being too slow to avoid it.

The next morning, he picked up the trail only to find it dribbled with blood. That gruesome trail led to a river and an ugly discovery.

The Chinese goldminer's body was mangled, chewed in half by one of the great saltwater crocodiles that frequented this locality. One of the gnarl-backed beasts was lurking, semi-submerged, in the river not a hundred yards away and Holmes knew he must not linger. Those fearsome reptiles were as fast on land as in water. Even at full strength, Holmes would be hard-pressed to outsprint the monster.

A quick examination of the body showed that the miner had died before making a meal for the brute. Other signs evidenced torture. Strips of skin had been sliced neatly from his face, arms and chest, as wide and as long as a shoelace. His expression was a rictus of terror. He appeared to have died of cardiac arrest after biting his own tongue near in half in a fit. Peculiar marks around the entry to his left ear were blurred by water and the tooth marks of some smaller carnivore.

Holmes made note of every salient fact, then backed swiftly away from the shore, alert for the crocodile and any of its lurking kin. As he drew away from the river's overpowering smell of rotting vegetation and dead flesh, Holmes heard a splash, a roar, then a gurgle, and knew that the poor man's remains would be found by no other.

Holmes sought new avenues of enquiry in Palmerston. What he discovered filled him with alarm and despair, but also determination. He'd sacrificed too much to lose this terrible game now.

Two days later, an elderly Chinese man walked stooped over through the docks. He was bent into an inverted hook, from his long, grey, pointed beard, over the curve of his bowed head, shoulders and back and to the spindly length of his legs. He was fast enough on his feet, however, darting through the throng of people and carts at the Port of Darwin, on his urgent mission.

The old Chinaman's sallow face was gaunt and watchful, but he ducked apologetically whenever any fellow bumped into him. Some of the Europeans bumped into him with blundering, uncaring strides and then demanded he apologise. He bowed and moved on. One tried to strike him with the back of a large hand, but he dashed aside, far more nimble than he looked. The churlish dockworker only succeeded in bashing his own hand on the side of a barrel.

Finally, the old man halted and backed into the minimal shade of a pile of crates and luggage. He pressed a sleeve to his face to carefully mop the sweat from his brow without smearing either paint or putty. This disguise was more difficult to manage in the tropical heat than was safe, but his options were limited.

The Port of Darwin docks thronged with sailors, merchants, traders and other human traffic, just as the berths were lined with clippers, barques, schooners and smaller vessels. Trimmed sails rose like liana-strewn and foliage-denuded trees from the decks of wooden sailing ships, iron hulls and the lighter steel vessels, too. Even on the steamships, the bare forest of masts stood tall, retained in case the fuel should run out on a long journey and the captain have to resort to the vagaries of wind and current. The creak of ropes and the slap of water against hulls mingled with the shouts of men and the cries of seabirds, as well as the groan of hemp and croak of metal emitted by the hoists and cranes, the crash and thump of shifting cargoes, and the rattle of carts bringing goods to and from the wharf. From where Holmes lurked, the stench of salt air, old fish, creosote, horse dung, guano and sweat intensified or grew fainter with the humidity and the uncertain breeze.

Sherlock Holmes observed the small cutter bobbing at the wharf and found at last the face he was searching for.

Colonel Sebastian Moran.

Holmes curled his long fingers into fists and pressed them against his thighs. He was itching to do that brute a severe mischief. Were it not for Moran, Watson would not be in danger.

Holmes made himself relax. He watched as Moran secured a berth on the vessel, carrying the scantest of luggage, a single small trunk, a wicker basket and a canvas bag, on board. Moriarty's last lieutenant appeared unconcerned that he might be under observation. Perhaps Moran thought he had lost

Holmes on the voyage from Borneo. It had been a near thing; Holmes had been a week behind in his pursuit.

He was always a week behind the man, devil take him, ever since that fortuitous – or rather, deeply unlucky – encounter in the Colony of Natal.

Immediately following the Reichenbach confrontation and his sudden decision to take advantage of its aftermath to disappear, Holmes had secretly liaised with Mycroft, who in turn liaised with international police forces, to finalise the Moriarty business. Then, having chosen to leave London and Watson, he found he desired a break from his old profession, too. Holmes travelled for a year, following whims under numerous personae, sometimes working in laboratories, sometimes on the stage. He spent several months in Tibet before travelling for most of a year through Asia. Africa followed.

In the Colony of Natal, he had by chance seen Sebastian Moran in secret conference with one of the Boers known to be conspiring against the British Government. Holmes had alerted the Queen's local agent, resulting in one agent with a cut throat and Moriarty's chief lieutenant still at large.

Holmes decided to run this quarry to earth, almost on an impulse. His purposeless wanderings had palled. The man who had never thought himself lonely before he lived with Doctor Watson in Baker Street felt the absence of his friend keenly. This last task, a reminder of their old adventures together, was at least something to do.

Holmes had sent the agent's false identity papers to Mycroft, with a salient report. Immediately after, he followed Moran across Africa, then by boat across the sea to India, across the Bay of Bengal and the Andaman Sea, overland to the South

China Sea and to Spain's Philippine Islands, and thence to Borneo. Always days or weeks behind, Holmes pursued Moran, glad to have a purpose again at last, though it was a stalemate game at best.

One thing had protected Holmes throughout the pursuit. For all that the general public was unaware of his alleged death – and Watson's return to his literary efforts kept the issue muddy – his fall to oblivion at Reichenbach was, in police and criminal circles, common knowledge. Their immediate acquaintances at Scotland Yard and in the British Government had been informed and word had spread, hurried along by Mycroft's timely whispers in the right ears.

Mycroft had questioned his brother's decision to disappear when fate offered him such an opportunity. He had conveyed to Sherlock the depth of Doctor Watson's mourning, but Holmes was steadfast. The death of Sherlock Holmes would protect Doctor and Mrs Watson from the vengeful attention of any of Moriarty's inner circle that had escaped; and it freed all three of them from a situation that had become untenable. The nature of that situation he had not described, although Mycroft had certainly deduced it.

When he left England, Sherlock Holmes certainly had no intention of ever returning. Were it not for the terrible mistake he'd made in Borneo, he'd doubtless have faded into lonely obscurity.

Holmes cursed the slip that had resulted in his exposure. After being so careful for so long, that wholly unforseen and unexpected encounter at the Pontianak docks had finally alerted Moran to the fact that Sherlock Holmes was not dead. Moran objected to this discovery, and to Holmes's stated intention to see Moran face justice for his crimes – whether by hanging or one-to-one battle – in the strongest terms.

Their encounter was short and brutal, culminating in Moran's escape on board a merchant clipper and Holmes spending three fretful days recovering from a knife wound to his thigh. Furious at his own carelessness, Holmes limped aboard a ship as soon as the injury allowed, to follow Moran south to Australia.

The second ship met with exceedingly inclement weather during the crossing, limping into Palmerston five days behind the clipper. Holmes expected Moran to be long gone, but found instead that the villain was making inquiries about a man recently departed for the great southern city of Melbourne. One of the people he had questioned was the unfortunate miner who had since made a meal for the crocodiles.

My game is hunting some other quarry, Holmes realised. It explained some things, but almost everything remained in darkness. Instead of wasting time in useless self-recrimination for failing to operate at his best – too steeped in melancholy and aimlessness since stealing away from John Watson – he determined to renew his intellectual and physical vigour and put an end to this business.

However, in retracing Moran's footsteps in Palmerston after the prospector's murder, Holmes had confirmed his fears via dreadful news that almost made his heart stop.

Moran had sent a telegram to Ronald Adair in London:

The Professor's opponent lives. Collect termination payment from his medical ally, or I'll return to settle all accounts.

The meaning of the threat was unequivocal. Frantic, Holmes had wired Mycroft, using their old code. The missive translated as:

Moran knows. I wire JW today. Despatch him to Melbourne, Victoria under agent's alias. Do not explain anything; that is for me.

Then he sent the old summons to Watson – though it took him a moment to command the courage and harden his heart to the necessity.

Nothing less than the threat to John Watson's life would have made him contact his old friend.

He hadn't been prepared for Mycroft's reply a day later: *Package sent to the June widower. Commission accepted.*

Holmes sorrowed for John's loss, but even had he known of Mary's death he wouldn't have returned to London, no matter how he longed to go, or to see Watson, or to resume the life they once had together. His conclusions regarding Watson and himself had been logical and inescapable. Mary's death did not change the fundamental fact that London had no future for him that he could bear to live with.

The whole situation was worse, even, than the debacle with Victor, almost twenty years ago.

John Watson would doubtless find himself another wife in due course, provided he lived long enough to find someone to court. At least the telegram and shipboard billet guaranteed him six weeks or more of safety.

When the good doctor arrived in Melbourne, well, that difficulty must be dealt with when the time came. Melbourne was the current destination of Moran's prey, but Moran had been chasing the fellow at least since Borneo. Who knew where the hunt would end? Where the chase would lead them next was not clear, though he'd formed some theories.

Perhaps the entire matter would be dealt with by the time Doctor Watson reached port.

Perhaps Watson would join him for a final adventure (Holmes couldn't help a sharp surge of hope at the idea, which he ruthlessly suppressed) before the doctor returned to his settled life in London, and Holmes went on to... whatever occupied his time.

As Holmes, in the character of the old Chinese man, watched Moran negotiate passage on the cutter, he considered his options. If he could be certain that Moran intended to travel straight to Melbourne, it might be better to travel with the Afghan cameleers overland south to Adelaide, there to take a train east. Unfortunately, he knew too little of Moran's own target. If that mysterious person knew that Moran was on his scent, he might depart on an unpredictable tangent, with Moran in pursuit, and they'd both be lost. The once great gold rush city was by no means guaranteed as a final destination – the crash following the land boom had devastated the city's economy in recent years. Its population was reputedly fleeing destitution in the direction of new gold strikes in Western Australia, or back to their many countries of origin. Whatever business Moran and his prey were involved in, Melbourne was an unlikely final destination.

No. The only thing was to continue trailing Moran while learning what he could of the primary quarry that led this merry chase across the world.

Satisfied that Colonel Moran had made his arrangements, and furthermore didn't know that Holmes was close on his trail, the detective resumed his stoop and retraced his steps. In an alley behind his unsavoury hotel, Holmes shrugged off the disguise, scraping the putty from his eyes, nose and cheeks, to reveal another disguise beneath – that of a dishevelled, inebriated Norwegian sailor, a variant on his previous alias, Sigerson. Slipping into the persona's mannerisms and language was like putting on a second skin, overlain now with slovenliness, despair and surly disappointment to create a new disguised self.

Holmes dismissed the fleeting thought that he'd grown used to being anybody but himself any more; or that he preferred disguises to travelling under his own identity; or that the name Sherlock Holmes had begun to feel as though it were a disguise too. He'd spent so long hiding so much, his own name felt as much a feigned character as anyone else he was these days.

Aging seaman Arvid Nilsen staggered into the hotel, seemingly drunk before lunch. A scrunched up copy of the day's *Northern Territory Times and Gazette* was in his fist. 'Still no work,' he muttered on the way past the desk to the back stairs, which took him to a tiny, cheap room.

Once there, he scoured the paper for a ship that would take him in the merchant clipper's wake towards Melbourne.

Towards, God willing, John Watson.

Sherlock Holmes felt the pull of hope, and the repulsion of it, too.

Summoning the doctor into this case had been his only option, to keep Watson safe, but Holmes could not imagine a scenario in which this reunion ended well.

Chapter Four

The steamship *Lenora Ann* set sail from Gravesend without incident on the 8th of September, 1893. Its final passenger, Dr Ormond Sacker, boarded half an hour before she weighed anchor. He remained within his on-deck first class cabin as the great ship began the first leg of its voyage, traversing the Atlantic to the Mediterranean Sea for the Suez Canal.

Doctor Watson sat in the cabin and stared at his unpacked luggage. The locked despatch box containing his case notes was within a larger trunk. A number of new notebooks were among his shirts, their pristine pages awaiting his commentary.

Mycroft Holmes and his agents had completed their work in exemplary fashion, with suitable clothing and toiletries neatly folded and efficiently stacked in the trunk. What items lacking in his wardrobe had been generously supplemented by the elder Holmes, and an appropriate advance had been made from the future sale of the practice. Watson had locked the excess in the despatch box. His service revolver was in the trunk, too. The basic tools of his trade were all present in his medical bag.

Watson tried to ignore his discomfort at having shed his mourning garb. He knew it was no betrayal of his wife, or of Holmes, and necessary to avoid the detection of the one who meant him harm – one of Moriarty's few remaining lieutenants, Mycroft Holmes had said.

'Ronald Adair?' Watson had questioned, 'But he was Holmes's chief informant.' A fellow who had become quite steeped in villainy for one so young.

'It appears that this fact remains unknown to Adair's former colleagues,' explained Mycroft Holmes, 'One assumes that a recent communiqué has set him to protecting his secret. Never fear, Doctor Watson. We shall have our eye on him. If we can prove the link with your failed assassins, he'll be incarcerated at Her Majesty's pleasure.'

'See that you do. I wouldn't care for Mrs Hudson or Wiggins to be subject to his ruthless caution, simply because they also knew Sherlock Holmes.'

'No, no, they shall be safe, as shall you. I have arranged everything and a special carriage will take you to your ship at Gravesend. I'm afraid, however, you'll have to shed your armband and ribbon, Doctor. The fewer clues as to your true identity, the better.'

The ship's horn blew as the *Lenora Ann* entered the English Channel's shipping lanes. Watson drew out his pocket watch to check the time. A little past 8 o'clock. Watson snapped the watch shut and rubbed his thumb over the case.

Holmes had deduced so much about his former life from the thing, though Holmes had missed as much entirely. It was good that the watch had been cleaned before Watson had shown it to him, or he may have seen much more. The cause of Henry's wretchedness, or that the watch had been sent to him from Australia, after poor Henry's lonely death at last of drink and grief. It was astonishing that Henry had retained a friend to send word of his passing and this, the last symbol of their sad family. Its arrival had been timely, for Watson had been near to making an unforgivable error that would surely have ended in disgrace and ruin, not to mention the dissolution of the friendship he held most dear. The watch reminded him of the consequences of acting on the same urges that were instrumental in his brother's downfall. Soon after, Mary had come into their lives. She'd seemed a God-sent sign of salvation.

Watson slipped the watch into its pocket and left his cabin, locking the door behind him, to stroll around the deck. His fellow passengers were scattering, some to their cabins, some to better vantage points to watch the shipping lanes. All were contemplating their futures as England slid away behind them, or striking up acquaintanceships which would last for the six week journey.

Six weeks was a significant improvement on Watson's previous experiences of this trip. In 1866, when 19-year-old Henry's dalliance with a Parisian artist named Luc had led their father to abandon his failing business interests in that elegant city, the sea voyage south had taken almost five months.

Had their mother lived, a great deal would have been different, but she had passed after a long illness in India when John was six years old. Then, he was used to running barefoot and free-spirited with the servants' children, his companions since his birth. The family had returned to England after her death, both boys learning to rein in their free ways to fit in at school, but their father became in his turn less reliable.

John and Henry, five years his elder, had been left largely to raise themselves while their father pursued venture after venture of varying degrees of lawfulness and with varying degrees of success. Both lads were voracious readers, the younger brother often seizing upon the elder brother's volumes, in English, German and French, supplementing their education with Goethe, Murger, Thackeray, the Brontes, Carlyle, Ruskin, Jean Paul and John Stuart Mill.

They left England for France when their father's erratic business affairs made the journey necessary, until in due course Henry's indiscretions had forced another rapid departure.

John, fourteen at the time and with his own shy affections equally divided between their cook's sweet daughter Manon and his best friend, the adventurous Remy, was horrified at his own narrow escape. Surely he'd have received the same thrashing as Henry if their father had known he and Remy had once tentatively kissed, mouth to exploring mouth.

However, running away to the Australian goldfields had not solved any of their family's financial or personal problems. The goldfields were already failing for many new prospectors. Henry Watson Senior – Harry to his friends and debtors – continued to have bad luck born of poor choices, leaving his sons to work his small Ballarat claim while he tried his luck further north in Queensland. Within two years, the older brother was not only in disgrace once more but in prison, and Watson the younger was being packed off to Britain to resume a gentleman's education, far from scandal. Their father had at least found enough gold to see to that.

Thus John Watson spent five more months at sea in a wretched, stinking, perilous sailing ship, in order to apply himself to learning how to be a common Englishman, to fit in at a boarding school and then at university, and after that the army, having learned his hard lessons in conformity.

The chief lesson among them was this: for a man to love and desire another man was to invite disgrace, death, ruin and despair.

That lesson had been flogged into his brother. It had destroyed his father's health. It had ensured that John Watson not once, ever in their friendship, declared that his love for Sherlock Holmes could be anything more than that of a close comrade. Sherlock Holmes, he knew, was too noble a man, and too reasoning a thinker, to reciprocate such dangerous affections.

Standing at the rails of the *Lenora Ann*, the man who now travelled as Dr Sacker regarded the horizon with unhappy speculation.

Despite Mycroft Holmes's assurances, doubt nagged at him. Who had known of the joking telegram that Holmes used habitually to send to him, apart from the staff of the telegraph office? Why should anyone choose to send such a communication?

Was the agent waiting in Melbourne an unknown man who had taken such a heartbreaking liberty with that message? Or had Sherlock Holmes somehow survived the fall into that dreadful abyss? Had he lived – only to abandon England, London, his brother and his friend, without word or pity?

Either solution lit a rage in him, and for all the long weeks of the sea voyage, that fire burned low but unfailingly.

*

The Norwegian sailor, Arvid Nilsen, worked his passage along the coast, the vessels he worked sometimes heaving to at jetties not a hundred yards from the cutter bearing Colonel Moran south. When Moran abandoned his ship, Holmes

45

likewise abandoned his to make enquiries, to learn Moran's next steps and to follow in them.

At ports along the coastline, Holmes's investigations led him to dead men. A merchant, a laundry worker, a cook and a miner: all but one of them Chinese.

Each and every man had been tortured, strips of narrow flesh cut from their bodies, when the bodies could be found. Each and every one with peculiar damage around one or both ear canals. Each and every one with unmistakable signs of having died in the most hideous fits of agony and terror, with lips drawn stiffly back from bared teeth, eyes starting from bruised sockets as though they beheld the devil himself in the last moments before death, and always swivelled in hideous watchfulness towards the damaged ear. Sherlock Holmes had seen many terrible deaths, but corpse after corpse displaying the depths of heart-bursting horror brought him singular unease and unsettled nights, for he was unable to deduce what Moran was inflicting upon these poor souls.

Holmes learned four things about the man that Moran pursued: he was a Chinaman; he'd been born twenty-odd years ago in the colony of Victoria; he carried a secret; his name was Li Ju-Long.

Holmes knew a fifth thing about Li Ju-Long; had known it from the moment he heard the name.

Li Ju-Long was a small but dangerous fish who had escaped the net set for Moriarty.

*

By the time the *Lenora Ann* had passed through the Suez Canal, Watson was settled in his routines on board. He spent much of his time writing in his cabin, though when sleepless

46

he'd pace the decks. The Indian Ocean crossing was less terrifying than the voyage around the Cape of Good Hope he remembered from his boyhood, although he recalled that exhilarating terror with some fondness too. He'd been wilder then, and the adventure of the storms and an encounter with the whale pod were more thrilling than fearful.

This late September afternoon, Watson turned the pages of his case notes and scrawled in one of the new books, highlighting what he could of the Moriarty-related cases. Some he'd transformed into tales for publication, having first extricated Moriarty's gang from the narrative. The counterfeiters' affair that cost that poor hydraulic engineer his thumb, and the incident of the beryl coronet were among them, cases that proved the Professor's gang were as ready to act against crown and state for gain, as against any common king of commerce. Watson had been meticulous in keeping those secrets safe, as both Holmeses had requested and insisted.

Jotting down the salient points refreshed Watson's memory of the details. Where he found Holmes's recorded comments or his own analysis in hindsight shed fresh light, Watson noted those as well. How useful such information would be was unclear, but he had weeks to fill and he couldn't spend it all stalking the deck and stewing over that cursed telegram.

Yet re-examining these private papers had its own difficulties. The notebooks contained case notes and sketches. At medical school, his study diagrams had been workmanlike, if not inspired. These books were another matter. The sketches of artefacts, crime scenes and wounds from their adventures were little better than his old diagrams; but those he'd idly drawn on blank pages and in the margins, of Holmes's face, his hands –

those were a confession in themselves. His despatch box was not kept under lock and key for the sake of their clients alone.

Watson was completing his notes on the unpublished business with the Pinkertons fellow and the murderous Molly Maguires when a sharp rap at his cabin door interrupted his revision. He bundled notebooks new and old into a pile and shoved them into the trunk, which he locked as he called out, 'A moment!'

He capped the ink and unlocked his cabin door to the fresh-faced young purser who saw to the needs of the passengers in this section of the ship.

'Pardon me, Doctor Sacker, but Doctor Pimm has asked for me to fetch you. He says he has need of your assistance.'

Watson fetched his bag and followed the boy, relocking the door behind him. This was the third occasion on which Pimm had sought him in a professional capacity. The old fellow was around sixty, a good twenty years older than Watson, and had trouble keeping his consulting room in order. Pimm reminded Watson very much of some of his lecturers at the University of London, many of whom had argued long and hard against the "preposterous notion of tiny animals making people sick". Watson was glad he'd always read outside the approved curriculum, and discovered for himself the revolutionary work of Lister, Koch and Pasteur, before a more formal introduction to their work on germ theory at Netley.

The little sick bay was too full of patients. Watson put that down in part to the fact that once more, Dr Pimm had failed to wash his hands with carbolic soap between clients and thereby generated more work. There was no excuse for such lack of hygiene in modern medicine.

'How may I be of assistance, Dr Pimm?'

Pimm waved to one of the waiting passengers with a scalpel smeared in blood and pus, used moments before to lance a boil that some unfortunate sailor had developed upon his neck. 'Administer Mrs Shearer with laudanum for her morning sickness, there's a chap.' He wiped the scalpel on his unclean apron and went to pierce the site again.

'Carbolic, Dr Pimm!' said Watson sharply. Pimm glared at him, but threw the blade into a dish for later cleaning, washed his hands appropriately, and picked up a second, clean instrument.

Watson examined Mrs Shearer, took her temperature, listened to both her and her baby's heartbeats, and ascertained the severity of her nausea.

'This is your first child, Mrs Shearer?'

The poor young woman nodded miserably.

'Well, you'll be glad to know that your nausea notwithstanding, you and your baby are both healthy and strong. There's no reason you will not remain so. Is your husband at hand?'

'Here, Doc,' said the worried gentleman by the door.

'Take your wife to the foredeck, wrap her in a blanket to keep her warm and let her sit a while in the fresh air. This nausea is as much seasickness as the effects of childbearing. Mrs Shearer, I'd like you to rest and take deep breaths, and keep your eyes on the horizon. It will hold its place even when the remainder of the ship does not. You'll find you're less dizzy before long. I'll send the purser with something for you to drink, as well as the recipe for future use. It's a simple infusion of lemon juice, honey, ginger root and mint. It'll settle you, I'm sure. When you've had enough sun and air, go to your cabin and rest. Mr Shearer, bring your wife some broth or some other plain fare. Come to see me again tomorrow if it doesn't effect any relief.'

The Shearers departed and Watson sent a purser to the galley with instructions for the infusion written on a piece of paper. He washed his hands and chose which patient to see next, based on need – that transpired to be the boy who had given himself a nasty rope burn while skylarking about in the lower rigging. Watson cleaned the wound, wrapping it first in a carbolised bandage and then a linen one.

'Keep it clean, there's a good lad. Come back tomorrow for a new dressing,' said Watson.

The remainder of Pimm's patients were despatched with similar care, and Watson took on the task of cleaning Pimm's instruments while the old fellow himself slumped in a chair.

'I'm retiring to my daughter's household once we reach Melbourne,' admitted Pimm, 'To become a gentleman of leisure in a more clement climate. I can't keep up with all of this. My memory isn't what it was. You seem to have the right of it though, young Sacker.'

Watson smiled. He hadn't been a "young" anyone for a good many years. 'I was an army doctor for a time,' he confessed, 'I believe the habits of organisation have rather stuck.'

'Well, I suppose you do have to deal with larger numbers in that work.'

'Indeed. The methodical set-up of a field hospital, from supplies to hygiene routines, is essential to saving lives. Triage becomes a great deal simpler, too.'

'No doubt. You were a surgeon?'

'Assistant surgeon, to begin, but a field surgeon too, until an enemy bullet saw an end to that career.'

'Ha, I bet you were glad of your well-organised hospital then, eh, Doctor Sacker?'

'Very much so, and of course of my orderly who carried me away from that slaughterhouse of a battlefield.'

'You must find private practice a relief after such an adventure.'

In truth, Watson found private practice immensely dull, save that brief period where his medical rooms were close to Paddington Station and he could occasionally revive his field surgery skills to assist rail workers who had met with industrial accidents. His best skills had often remained unused, except when he'd worked with Holmes and his many strange and dangerous cases.

'What was that treatment you offered the lady? The one with child?' Pimm continued, 'You didn't give her the laudanum.'

'Oh, it's a concoction the Indian medicine men used to give to the servants' wives, and sometimes to the English women. It was very efficacious. I prefer to reserve the stronger medicines for more pressing cases, when we have no means of replenishing our stocks.'

He'd been fascinated by the work of the Indian practitioners of Ayurvedic medicine in his youngest years. Their remedies hadn't cured his mother of her cancer, but neither had the best treatments of the British establishment.

'You were in India with the army?'

51

'As a child, too. My father worked for a time with the East India Company, though we managed to escape the crisis of '57 unharmed.'

Watson wondered that he was talking to this stranger so freely of his past. But then, he was lonely, and however negligent Pimm could be, exchanging a few words with a colleague for a short while made him less lonely.

'I first grew interested in medicine from observing the effect of their native remedies. My interest was cemented some years later, on a similar voyage to this in fact, when my father took the family to Australia. When I wasn't climbing ropes like the Godfrey boy who was in earlier, I loitered about the doctor's quarters and watched him work.'

Those formative encounters in childhood had sparked the young John Watson's thirst for healing. Reading to ill passengers – at the urging of the shipboard doctor who thought he might put the eager lad to *some* use – proved he had, at least, a soothing bedside manner.

'What a life of adventure you have led, Doctor Sacker!'

Watson became acutely aware that he'd said too much, and knew too little about Dr Pimm.

'Oh, a little travel, and some very unfortunate encounters with danger. You're quite right that private practice is a great relief from such unpleasantness.'

Watson finished wiping the surfaces, ensured his own and the shipboard surgery's instruments were clean, the soiled aprons were bundled away for the laundry service and that his hands and face were washed. He smoothed a knuckle over his moustaches.

'Well, good afternoon, Doctor Pimm.'

'Good afternoon, Sacker. I trust I may call on you again, if the need arises?'

Watson had the impression that Dr Pimm would prefer to begin his retirement immediately, and gathered that Pimm had taken on this role of ship's doctor to save a fare on passage to the colony. Watson had things he'd rather be doing himself, but he found that the straightforward work in this sick bay helped to clear and soothe his troubled thoughts.

'Of course you may, Doctor Pimm.'

That night, Watson dreamed of Holmes's hands, and of being touched by them: holding his own at first, but then roaming all over his still-clothed body. Then of long, clever fingers insinuating themselves between the gaps, under vests and his drawers, brushing warm against his skin. Watson climaxed in his sleep, and woke at once, face damp with… with perspiration, he told himself. Not tears. Naught but perspiration.

As he cleaned himself with a handkerchief, Watson, feeling exposed – though to none but himself – could not help but consider the dream.

Watson had loved Mary, but he had loved Holmes too – as a friend, but also with longing and desire. He remembered listening to those men in the nearest tent, when he was a boy in Ballarat, both aroused and reassured by the soft sounds he heard. It seemed to him that those men had been loving. His own brother was such a man. A good and kind man. A good brother. Society may perceive the physical love of one man for another as perversion, but Watson's understanding of it was kindness.

But when Henry was discovered, society's view won. The consequences for Henry were horrible. Watson knew he must keep the vice in himself well hidden or face a similar fate, but he didn't think himself a sinner because of it. He'd kept such feelings hidden from a man who had no time for them, but Holmes had been a beautiful man, in mind, body and heart, and worth loving.

Watson placed the soiled handkerchief on the little table beside the bed, ready to wash in the morning. He fell asleep, and did not dream.

*

Holmes spent a restless night in his billet as the ship raced southward.

Sherlock Holmes had never trained himself not to want, or not to care. But after Victor Trevor he had trained himself not to succumb to those things. He noted his feelings, his desires, then set them aside for the sake of the clear reasoning that was his goal and purpose in life as he pursued the singular and often outré role he'd assigned to himself.

Meeting Victor at university had drawn Holmes – with a reputation already for oddness and perceived coldness of manner – into the possibilities of the heart. They were each other's shameful secret, though Victor found him so shameful, in fact, that he would not linger in bed after they had been satisfied. Holmes taught himself not to mind, or at least to pretend so, and accepted less than he hoped for as more than enough. Things were already souring with Victor by the time he visited Victor at home, culminating in the story of the *Gloria Scott* and the death of Mr Trevor Senior.

Those eighteen preceding months had been strange and dangerous and yet happy, but the confusion and devastation over their ending had taught Holmes that sentiment was for fools.

Nothing had tempted him to think otherwise, until Stamford had brought a battle-worn ex-army surgeon to the laboratory.

John Watson had been, and remained, Holmes's greatest challenge.

All the discipline he could muster wouldn't banish the fantasies that came to Holmes on the loneliest of nights. Most revolved around the good doctor's hands, which had tended Holmes's wounds and illnesses; his voice, which heaped praise where others had only expressed alarm, incredulity or scorn; his wonderful, warm laughter, shared with him and not directed at him; his brown eyes, which though they failed to observe most things that didn't fall within his medical purview, yet saw enough, and danced with humour and appreciation too. Even Watson's *golden brown hair*, for God's sake. He'd wondered how it would feel to his touch, just as he wondered how Watson's moustache might feel against his body.

This night, lying exhausted on an unforgivingly hard bed, Holmes employed his usual techniques to banish such thoughts, but they persisted on a wave of painful awareness: *I'll see him soon.*

And so Holmes imagined a warm hello and the smile that crinkled Watson's eyes and made his moustache lift in a way that was inexplicably charming. Then more: he imagined Watson's hands holding his and his voice murmuring, 'Oh, my dear boy, it is unspeakably good to see you.'

Holmes imagined an impossible kiss, then many more, all over his face, and his body, and himself reciprocating, his lavish attentions welcomed.

He imagined himself afterwards in Watson's arms, head pillowed on his broad chest in the way that Victor had always denied him.

Holmes also knew that none of this would happen. He knew that imagining it, with all the power of detail at his command, would bring him nothing but grief.

Yet he imagined.

Then he cursed being in love and not knowing how to undo it.

And he held his unrequited love close in his heart, for it was the only thing that gave him warmth in his loneliness.

Days later, Holmes thought he'd overtaken Moran when his vessel bypassed Port Macquarie, but they found each other at Sydney – a brief glimpse across the docks. Moran grinned savagely at him and shouted:

'Your pal has met his maker, and so soon will you!'

Holmes knew him for a liar, but once he lost Moran in the heaving, close-packed crowd, he wired Mycroft. Mycroft confirmed that Watson was on board the *Lenora Ann*.

Holmes was heartsick, but there was nothing for it but to continue his pursuit of Moran. If the *Lenora Ann* arrived and Watson had not survived the journey after all, there would be a bloody reckoning.

*

Watson wrapped his waterproof tightly closed and clutched his bag. The storm battered the *Lenora Ann* on the great heaving surface of the sea. The prow rose up like a horse shying from a serpent before lurching down again, ready to kick its hooves and throw its fragile human riders into the roiling waves. He ought to have been sheltering in his cabin, where he had already packed away his possessions against the expected violence, but when Mrs Shearer's husband begged him for help, Watson could hardly refuse, or expect Dr Pimm to make his way across the spray-slicked decks to their cramped belowdecks cabin.

Mrs Shearer's fall had caused tenderness and some bleeding, but she and the babe were in no immediate danger, provided she could stay in her bed. The heaving sea made that difficult, so Watson and Mr Shearer tied scarves to the bed-frame, giving her something to anchor her position. She was further packed into the mattress with pillows and bundled clothing. Mr Shearer was charged with ensuring all loose items were stowed in their trunks, and the trunks shoved hard into the corner. Watson dared not give Mrs Shearer a sleeping draught while the ship lurched with such unpredictable energy, but he did what he could for the couple.

Now he made for his own cabin to survive the rest of the storm as best he may. The weather had turned from coarse to ugly in the interim, and he congratulated himself on not bringing his hat, for surely he'd otherwise lose it to the storm.

The afternoon sky was night-dark with black clouds and driving rain as Watson gripped ropes with his free hand and hauled himself towards his cabin. Once or twice he dimly saw crew members working in their sealskin gear and streaming sou'westers. He sent up a prayer that they'd maintain their hold, and then another that he'd maintain his own.

He was almost at his door when he perceived, through the black curtain of rain, a kitchenhand who had boarded at Suez and whom he'd recently treated for a nasty burn.

'Delancey, lad,' he shouted, 'You should be below!'

Delancey grinned at him in a most unfriendly manner. 'As soon as I'm done with this chore, Doctor Watson!'

The words were whipped away by the wind, and Watson doubted if he'd heard aright – but the boy lunged at him, a fish-gutting knife in his fist, and there was no mistaking Delancey's intent.

Watson threw his medical bag up as a shield, deflecting the blow as the prow lifted. He was tipped against the walls of cabins arrayed behind him. He staggered as the prow plunged down into the boiling sea once more, and Delancey came at him and pinned him to the deck.

'The sea's been too quiet to make an easy end of you, since I found you on board,' Delancey said, close to Watson's ear as he pressed his advantage and the blade of his knife close to the doctor's throat, 'Until it seems the spirit of the Professor sent me a storm to do you in. Adair will be happy he thought to spread word for us to keep lookout. It'll be riches and praise for me, when I get word out I did for you! And it'll teach that bastard Holmes there's no hiding from our revenge!'

Watson twisted under the lad, who was young and strong, but the doctor was more heavily set and experienced. He certainly knew better than to waste his breath on crowing over a victory that was not yet attained.

Holding the blade away from his throat with a desperate grip around the lad's wrist, he jabbed the cold-numbed fingers of his free hand hard into Delancey's throat, into the vulnerable point under the hinge of his jaw where nerve endings gathered beside the temporomandibular joint. As Delancey cried out and recoiled, Watson released his wrist and punched up, knuckle jutting out, into the man's temple.

The prow lurched up, tumbling them over one another, awash with the freezing wave that scoured the deck. Watson flung out both arms desperately, seeking purchase. His hands tangled with the ropes fastening a lifeboat to the deck and he held on.

Delancey, mouth open in a terrible shriek that Watson couldn't hear for the storm, tumbled overboard – so much flotsam.

When the deck tilted the other way, Watson scrambled for his cabin door, splashing through the remaining wash of saltwater. Though his hands were rope-burned and numb, he managed to unlock the door, fling himself within and kick the door shut.

He sat shivering on the floor in his sodden clothes, his body braced between his cot and the wall against the heaving of the steamship.

The storm, as many storms do, blew itself out within half an hour. Watson rose stiffly and dared to open his door onto the glistening decks.

The evening sky was clear and bright with twinkling stars. The crew called to each other in the cold air, like nightbirds hooting their roosts to one another. It might be morning before the crew discovered they'd lost one of their number to the storm. Watson decided not to enlighten them. He no longer knew whom he could trust.

From his doorway, Watson was astonished to see his medical bag tangled among the ropes of the lifeboat that had saved him. He collected it and returned to his room to sort through broken vials and disarrayed instruments so that he could treat the rope burn on his right hand and the small cut to his neck. He peeled off his drenched suit, shoes and underthings, wrapped himself in every one of the cabin's scratchy woollen blankets and poured a nip of brandy to stave off the chill.

It'll teach that bastard Holmes there's no hiding from our revenge!

Watson swallowed another nip of brandy, but his rekindled anger was much more effective at returning the heat to his blood.

*

When Sherlock Holmes arrived in Melbourne, five and a half weeks after leaving Palmerston, he scoured the newspaper columns, lurked in the coffee palaces and eavesdropped in the public houses until he found a thread and followed it. Shortly thereafter, he struck up a casual acquaintance with, and bought a drink for, one Mr Browne, who had recently left hospital after treatment for a broken thumb.

From Browne, Holmes learned that one of Moran's victims, Mr Alistair McLeod – an Australian-born Scotsman – was still alive, though it was unclear how much good the discovery would do his investigation.

Mrs McLeod had gone mute from terror, said Browne, and admitted no visitor to her home. This he had learned as he lay in his cot beside Mr McLeod, when he overheard the nuns speaking. McLeod himself thrashed about in a fever on a hospital bed, raving and weeping.

The hour was much too late to gain access to the Sisters of Charity hospital where the poor deranged man was sickening. Nonetheless, Holmes left Browne with a half bottle of ale, and crept his way around the grounds. Mr McLeod was, he determined, alive and, due to the calming effects of laudanum, asleep. There would be no more data from that source until the morning. The muteness of Mrs McLeod couldn't be challenged until he learned her address – another chore for the morrow.

The *Lenora Ann* was due into port the next morning. Doctor Watson would be aboard – *must* be aboard – and surely would join with him in this last case.

Chapter Five

When last John Watson had arrived on these shores, in 1866, the sailing ship had berthed at Queen's Wharf on the Yarra River. The shore had teemed with those seeking their fortunes in the goldfields of this rich colony. That the Watsons had met with ill fortune was not due to the colony's deficiencies.

Now the *Lenora Ann* was tied at the Victoria Docks, a new facility by a railyard, and the frantic, optimistic activity of the goldrush years had dampened to a more prosaic air of dogged, begrimed determination. The boom had come to bust, and the shine of Melbourne had been tarnished by greed, poverty and even penury. It was hardly a wonder that the mysterious agent had so easily and on such short notice found Watson a single berth on the outward-bound journey.

Watson caught sight of Mr and Mrs Shearer – the latter round-bellied and in excellent spirits – waving farewell. He saluted an acknowledgement with his now-healed right hand. The loss of Delancey during the storm had occasioned solemnity among the crew, and Watson had kept his knowledge of the lad's fate to himself. He couldn't see that he had other enemies in the remaining crew, but neither had he been aware of Delancey's ill-intent, and he thought it best to keep his silence. After all, the lad had certainly been lost at sea, and knowledge of his perfidy wouldn't be a comfort to his friends and family.

Watson engaged a carriage to take him and his luggage to Collins Street, where Mrs Gallagher's guesthouse awaited him. The carriage took him past several grand buildings, completed just as the economy had crashed, the sumptuous buildings standing as monuments to hubris.

They were passed several times by horseless, almost silent trams running east and west on Collins Street. Watson studied them with interest, and asked his driver after their mechanism. The driver pointed out the furrows in the street, under which cables ran between far flung wind-houses. A gripman in the tram, yelled the driver to his passenger, used a tool to grab onto the cable, which then hauled the vehicle along. 'They go a good clip, Dr Sacker,' shouted the man, 'Best be careful crossing the street.'

The horses carried on up the gentle slope of the street, past crowds gathered at the prettily tiled entrance to a place marked the Block Arcade, towards a hill. To the left was The Melbourne Club, its stern frontage a fortress from calamity for its well-heeled members. Beyond and opposite that exclusive club was a cobbled lane. The driver turned down this, leaving the wide road and imposing facades for a more crowded cluster of buildings and apartments. The driver reined his horse to a standstill before one of these with a door painted in chipped but cheerful green. For an extra consideration, the driver assisted Watson in fetching his luggage to the front door.

Away from the immediate grandeur of Collins Street, Watson was aware of a terrible smell. He'd read that the city still did not have sewerage, and here the open drains were the proof of it. He held a handkerchief over his nose and thanked the heavens that no rain fell to overflow the filthy gutters.

Mrs Gallagher answered the door. A lady more unlike Mrs Hudson he could never hope to meet. This woman was tall and spare, dressed in a paint-smeared smock and with her long hair falling from its pins. Some of the flyaway locks were also smeared in paint of varying hues. The lady held a brush in one hand as she perused – and promptly stained – the letter of introduction he gave her in the other.

'Ah, Doctor Sacker, I've been expecting you. I trust the voyage went well for you. I've not been so far out at sea, having been born a native of Australia and spent my life here, but I've been on the bay once or twice. The sunsets as seen from a yacht on Port Phillip Bay are lovely, though very difficult to catch on canvas at the time. The decks do heave so. My friend, Mr Norris, manages it with a clever amount of tying down of his easel, and he claims the way the paint sprawls is an admirable reflection of the motion of the decks, but I feel it makes the art seem seasick. I suppose it may be claimed that this makes it a perfectly affecting piece of art, to make the viewer as nauseated with the painting as the artist felt on painting it, though I prefer a less literal impression myself....' All this she said while guiding Watson, carrying his cane and medical bag, up the stairs to the first storey, while a muscular porter heaved the trunk up behind them. 'And here you are. I'm up a further set of stairs there, with my little studio in the attic, and I must return to my painting – an exhibition is to be held at Buxton's next week, and while it seems no-one is left who can afford to purchase a painting, I suppose it can't hurt to present. Streeton will be there, and Bulldog Roberts, I'm told, and they always bring in the art lovers and the speculators. It seems anything out of Heidelberg draws a crowd, and so I hope my work might at least be witnessed by someone. Here is your key, breakfast is at eight in the parlour downstairs, and we generally have a cold collation in the evening. Please come and go as you like, though mind I

64

won't have drunkenness, and don't mind Pippin, he can't help his face and is much friendlier than he looks.'

Watson looked down in surprise at the chubby pug who had appeared at the landlady's feet. Its muzzle was scarred, giving it a fierce aspect, but its wagging tail thumped on the floor and it panted grinningly in a perfectly friendly manner. Watson bent to pat the creature. The tail-thumping and panting increased accordingly.

'See, you are excellent friends already,' declared Mrs Gallagher. She disappeared up the stairs, the cheerfully ugly Pippin at her heels. The porter had deposited the luggage in his room. Watson pressed a coin into the fellow's hand. The fellow tugged the brim of his cap in thanks and clattered down the stairs again.

In his room, Watson shook his head at the carelessly friendly welcome. What his next move should be was a mystery, but the immediate future was best spent unpacking. Then he'd consider how to seek the agent that had sent for him. *If agent it was, and not...*

That thought soured his mood. He set it aside and opened first his valise with his immediate necessaries. From it, he set out his toiletries – comb and razor blade, a tin of hair wax and his toothbrush. He poured water from the waiting jug into the basin and washed his hands and face.

Watson turned at a tap on the door as he was drying his face. 'Yes?'

'Doctor Sacker?' The voice rang with an accent he couldn't quite place, though it seemed to hail from beyond the North Sea. Finland or Sweden.

'Who wishes to know?'

'I come with information from a Mr Mycroft Holmes, sir.'

The agent had come to him. He supposed it saved some time, though there remained the possibility that this agent didn't come from Mycroft Holmes at all but from their unnamed enemy. Watson took up the gun from his valise. 'Come in, then.'

A scruffy sailor, the worse for years and probably drink, stood in the threshold. The seaman stared at the gun. 'Begging your pardon, Doctor Sacker,' he said, 'My name is Arvid Nilsen. Mr Holmes asked me to make certain you were arrived safe and sound. He said to tell you as a sign that you're safe with me that the true name of the client in that business with the coronet, which was in fact a bracelet, was the Duke of Connaught and Strathearn.'

That royal connection with the delicate business so otherwise altered beyond recognition in the published story was known only by Holmes, his brother, himself, and of course the Duke. Watson nodded and replaced the gun in his bag, thinking that the sailor's accent was perhaps Norwegian, and that under the cadences of those vowels and consonants it sounded familiar in a way that made his heart flutter and his spine crawl with misgivings.

'Give me one moment,' Watson began, 'I have just arrived…'

He heard movement, and saw the sailor Arvid Nilsen disappearing before his eyes – cap gone, posture straightening, the man's gnarled and curled hands flexing elegantly to sweep his hair back and to smooth out unruly eyebrows.

'I am unspeakably glad to see you safe arrived at last, Watson!' Sherlock Holmes greeted him genially. His smile was bright, his eyes twinkling as always. Though he was rake thin and looked to have been using himself too freely, he was in so many respects the Sherlock Holmes of old.

Watson did not reach out to take Holmes's offered hand in greeting. He stood as though frozen by the Gorgon, his eyes round, his lips pressed hard together. One side of his mouth dimpled as he bit the inside of it against precipitate comment.

Watson's mind was blank and crowded all at once. He felt as he had in the moments after the Jezail bullet tore into his shoulder at Maiwand, when the cries of his wounded and dying comrades around him faded into the rushing of blood in his own ears, the torment from shattered bone, muscle and cartilage reducing his lively intellect to a traumatic pinpoint. So many of his company falling and dying, and he dying with them, soundless in that awful rush. And after the hush, the pain again, as the terror of dying gave way to the agony of *not* dying, as Murray dragged him to safety and brought him to aid.

Seeing Holmes in front of him now was both things: the roaring hush of dying and the awful agony of surviving.

He is alive, thank God, thank you God, oh thank you merciful God, alive.

He lied to me. He did not trust me. He let me believe he was...

I should thrash him for what he has done.
Oh, but he lives.
What do I do? What do I do?

Holmes's open hand had closed and he stood in dignified silence by the door. 'Well, of course, it is a great shock. I do apologise, Watson, my good fellow. Pray, be seated. We have much to discuss.'

Watson's reply was to turn his back and seek the few items he'd already unpacked. He opened his valise carefully and stowed his toiletries within. He looked for his coat, realised he still wore it, and closed the bag.

'We may attend to your luggage later,' said Holmes in a crisp voice.

Watson placed his medical bag upon the bed and peered into it. He couldn't remember why he'd done so and closed it. He turned, caught sight of Holmes, and frowned. He took out his pocket watch – not merely a family heirloom but a constant reminder of how he must conduct himself. He was used to that *frisson* of regret and loathing on seeing it. It had survived the sea voyage, mostly by virtue of the fact he hadn't taken it with him into the storm the night Delancey had struck – but remembered now that the current o'clock was of little use to him without a destination.

'I suppose I must find the local newspaper and peruse the shipping news if I'm to determine when I may depart again for England.'

Holmes's friendly smile vanished. He appeared if anything paler and more gaunt than before. 'You have only now arrived, Watson!'

'Yes. But as there is no reason to stay, I shall return and inform your brother that you are not, after all, smashed to pieces at the bottom of the Reichenbach Falls.'

'Mycroft already knows this, naturally.'

Watson went very still. 'Of course. Of course he does. I must seem very dull to you, to not have realised. To not have...' He grit his teeth and averted his eyes. 'Well, then, the matter stands as it did. I believe I have a word or two I must exchange with your brother.'

Holmes didn't move. Or rather, his feet twitched, and so too his hands, as though about to move, but something stayed him by the door. 'The next vessel for London doesn't depart for three days. There's no hurry, Doctor Watson. Perhaps, however, you would accompany me to the hospital, for there is a man there who appears raving mad and your medical opinion would mean much to my investigation.'

'Would it?' Watson's gaze finally met that of his old friend's.

'It would,' said Holmes.

They regarded each other across a chasm.

'I do believe that the colony has medical professionals of its own which may be of better service to you.'

'Of service, possibly, though not of *better*.'

Watson's gaze intensified into an accusation, and everything unsaid in that look was understood perfectly by the other man. In the end, Watson spoke, regardless.

'I should think,' said Watson stiffly, 'That if you had at all valued my services, I would not have been allowed to believe you dead these last two and a half years. I should *think* that I might have been of service to your investigations *then*. I should *think* that I deserved better at your hands than this appalling deception.'

'My leaving so abruptly had nothing to do with your value as a colleague,' said Holmes waspishly, 'I sought to protect you and your good wife.'

'I did not ask for your protection.'

'Yet you need it. Since Moran unfortunately discovered that I'm alive, there have been three attempts on your life.'

'Four,' Watson corrected him, 'Another occurred on the *Lenora Ann*, though he was ill prepared and, frankly, an amateur.'

Holmes pursed his lips gravely. 'You have been very lucky in your escapes.'

'Some might not consider it *luck*,' growled Watson, 'But tell me, is there a better reason for this cruel charade than *my protection*?'

'It was necessary I vanish and seem to be dead so that I could continue my work. Moriarty was not the only man who had sworn my death…'

'And yet Mycroft knew the truth. Did you believe me less capable of keeping your secret than your brother? You think so little of me?'

Holmes's grey eyes flashed angrily, then softened with a sorrow that Watson couldn't fathom or explain. 'No, Watson. The decision was made abruptly when I realised the unusual opportunity which had presented itself. My departure was not premeditated. I confess I fully expected to meet my end at Moriarty's hands. I determined not to mind it, provided I might ensure the end was mutual. I was surprised and I will say relieved that I won through after all.'

'And how came you alive from that dreadful chasm? Or were you never in it?'

'I was never in it, as you surmise, though it was a near thing. Moriarty, secure in the belief in my imminent destruction, kindly allowed me to write my farewell to you – please, do not doubt that the letter was genuine – but I was able to employ those Japanese martial arts which you know I practise. In the end, it was he who fell. Before his body broke upon the rocks, I realised that were I to vanish and become a ghost, as it were, I could at last free the world from those dangerous enemies who would destroy me, and you too, if they but had the chance. So I stole away, unseen, by climbing the rocky wall behind me. It was no mean feat and I nearly joined the Professor in the chasm after all, with one or two near slips. I found safety upon a ledge at last, however, and watched as you investigated my purported murder…'

'You *watched* me?' Watson's tone was dangerous, hard with a rage that lay thick upon the hurt beneath it.

Holmes faltered. 'I was trapped upon the cliff until I could be on my way. I could in no way risk being seen alive, for this opportunity was unique.'

Watson's face was white but for two hectic splotches on his cheeks. His moustache fairly bristled. 'Oh, I quite see. I quite understand the necessity of allowing me to investigate your murder, and get it all wrong, as usual. I imagine it afforded you some amusement on your precarious ledge while I read your note and called for you and wept for my dead friend.'

'I in no wise found it amusing.'

'Well, that is something, I suppose, for I know that *I* did not.'

'How you could think I would be so callous at your expense…'

'And yet you were. You have been. Even if it were a spur of the moment decision, Holmes, *you might have contacted me to correct my error*. It has been some *years*, after all.'

'I thought to do so. Often, truly,' he confessed. Then his face set sternly. 'But it was out of the question.'

'I see. You believe I would have betrayed you.'

'Watson, you would have wished to follow me abroad...'

'And abandon Mary? My practice? For *years*? You overstate your influence, Holmes. If it were not that my poor Mary had died, you wouldn't find me here now.'

At once, Holmes's grey eyes averted. When next he spoke, all brittleness was gone from his tone and he spoke as gently as he'd ever done to any deeply troubled client.

'I do, my dear fellow, offer my most sincere apologies, and condolences too. I know you're angry, but I acted as I saw best at the time. I was so very sorry to learn of your tragic loss. The news only came to me after I sent you my telegram. Had I known, I would not have been so...' He failed to find a word to describe or justify the apparent levity of the missive. 'Please, Watson, if you must return to England and be angry with me for all time, then you have the right and you have cause. But since you must necessarily wait the days until a ship departs, won't you visit this man with me? I can't be certain that the threat to your life will be neutralised until the case is solved. It would grieve me if they succeeded in their murderous plans now, after all our efforts.'

Watson hardly knew what to say in the face of Holmes's clear sincerity. He had no doubt that Holmes was concealing information from him – as he was ever wont to do. Yet there was some honest plea in this, and Holmes's concern for his wellbeing was not feigned.

He closely regarded Holmes, who had schooled his expression to a mask, and tried to apply the methods which Holmes had so often tried to teach him, alongside his own skills as a physician.

Holmes was pale and too thin, his skin sallow, the whites of his eyes dull, the skin under them dark and the lines around them more pronounced. The bristles of his unshaven jaw were speckled with grey among the dark. His mouth, always firm, crinkled at the corners with the effort of maintaining his neutral expression. His fingers betrayed the very slightest tremor.

Holmes had deliberately allowed Watson, and therefore the world, to believe he'd died in Switzerland, ostensibly to protect himself and, by extension, his friend, from attempts upon their lives. Someone had learned that Holmes lived and since then Watson had escaped death on four separate occasions. There was no telling how many attempts had been made upon Holmes himself. For all that this was not the sole motivation for the deception – Watson was certain that something else lay behind the prevarication he sensed in Holmes's tone – it was a compelling one and demonstrably accurate.

Holmes, Watson concluded, was exhausted; was not entirely well; and was genuinely concerned for Watson's safety. Surely his own as well, although he hadn't mentioned it. This much Watson could divine was true. All else was a question.

Watson decided on the spot that having come halfway across the world to assist in the final eradication of Moriarty's gang, the least he could do was see it through.

'You may have my assistance on this last case, if you wish it,' he said coolly.

'It is safest, I think,' said Holmes, who then led the way down into the Melbourne streets.

Chapter Six

The wide, sunlit street rolled and swayed under Watson's feet as he walked through Melbourne, his medical bag held as a barrier between him and Sherlock Holmes. He knew the perceived motion was his inner ear playing tricks upon his balance after six weeks at sea. Yet it reflected that other turmoil, too.

Holmes was alive.

The detective strode along the path, an arm's length away from him, his eager expression and sharp eyes as keen as ever while on the trail of their quarry, whoever that might be. Since their argument at the lodging house, Holmes had been careful to hide all traces of emotion. Watson was not sure he managed that feat so well himself, for he was so full of tumult he was hard pressed to say which raw feeling was uppermost. The part of him that exulted in Holmes's survival rubbed roughly alongside the part that was deeply wounded to have been allowed to mourn so unnecessarily for so long. The kinder part of him that informed the medical man and the friend longed to make Holmes sit and to examine and treat him for the clear signs of exhaustion and poor health; yet the less generous element of his soul declared that Holmes deserved his suffering.

Nevertheless, from time to time in their swift traversing of the city, Watson was aware of Holmes looking sidelong at him. Assessing him, as was his habit, and saying nothing, which was not.

Watson longed to bridge the space between them, to walk with his arm looped through Holmes's crooked elbow, as they had rambled through London in the past. He also longed to shake Holmes until his teeth rattled and to demand, *how could you have done this? To leave me all these years, and now behave as if it were nothing?*

Holmes's assertion that he'd left for Watson's protection and maintained his pretence of death for the same reason rang hollow. In any case, how dare Holmes make that decision for him? And the very idea that he'd have flown to Holmes's side was preposterous. It was not as though all Holmes had to do was snap his fingers, and there Watson would be.

Except, here I am, curse him.

Watson glared at his own shoes as they trod the Melbourne footpath, half a world away from his Kensington home.

I would have followed him. I'd have left Mary, London, everything, to fly to any corner of the world to be with him. It doesn't matter that he doesn't love me as more than a friend. If he ever loved me that far at all.

Yet had he ordered me to stay, I would have obeyed, however reluctantly. There is some other reason for his leaving and his silence – so my reasoning tells me. He took all decision from me, and took himself away.

Perhaps he knew. Knows. *Perhaps he left in that abrupt way to be rid of an unwanted regard. It would still be a cruel trick to have played upon me, for I never would have let my attachment cause him discomfort or shame. I guarded rigidly against any such thing for all the years I was single. I married a dear woman who deserved a better husband to prevent any hint of impropriety. I never asked him to requite me. So it was unspeakably cruel to let me think him dead.*

76

Watson walked on in his confused and angry misery, saying nothing.

The strained silence continued east to the hill and northward past the grand Parliament Building, which appeared oddly unfinished, obviously lacking a dome to complete the look of the edifice – an architectural embellishment perhaps abandoned after the crash of '91. They had to make way for traffic, including the cable trams that flowed, silent but for the creak of wood, along the street.

Ahead, at the junction of three roads, was the statue of the doomed explorers Burke and Wills. Even as a boy, Watson had not had much sympathy for them. They had great hearts, no doubt, but hardly any brain between them, to have attempted to carry a writing desk deep into the wilderness, and then to have disdained the good advice given to them by the natives. After arguments with other boys in the diggings that came to blows more than once, he'd learned to keep those opinions to himself. Henry had stood up for him. As a result, John had needed to bind up both their wounds. His first real doctoring.

'We shall be at the hospital soon. Do you wish to know nothing about the case?'

Watson came back to the present. He resisted a snipe of *I was waiting for you to see fit to share the intelligence, as usual* as unhelpful, though it took effort. 'Who is this poor man we are about to visit, then, and why is it of concern to your investigation?'

'I have these last few months been in pursuit of Colonel Sebastian Moran, whom I once mentioned to you as a confederate of Professor Moriarty's,' Holmes reported, 'Although he only became aware of my pursuit in Borneo – and

I apologise again for the danger that my carelessness has brought to you.'

Watson did not reply, lest another argument ensue.

'Moran, I learn, has himself been in pursuit of a man named Li Ju-Long, who was an up-and-coming felon in the gang's ranks. Li is Australian-born, and it's in this country he developed an acquaintance with the young Ronald Adair, when Adair's father was governor of the colony of Victoria. They met, I have ascertained, by chance at an opium den where Li worked; Adair had business dealings with the owner, supplying opium to wealthier clients who'd rather indulge their vices at home. Adair already had a flair for gambling in the two-up rings by then. Li introduced him to other low houses where they gambled. Whether Adair introduced Li to Moriarty's gang then or later is not clear. They made enough trouble, however, that Adair's father decided to return the family to England in the hope of taming his wayward son.' Holmes shrugged, as if to say "so much for that".

'Li seems to have followed Adair to London. They were both soon known to be juniors in the ranks of Moriarty's schemers, and reported to Moran. We were able to levy threats against Adair, as you know. In strict confidence and in fear for his life, Ronald Adair provided intelligence that helped us bring the whole business crashing down. His part as a Judas remains unknown to his surviving confederates, but if Moran catches up with Li Ju-Long, that ignorance may not continue. Li escaped the net – perhaps warned by Adair. I'm certain that if Moran knew of Adair's betrayal, Adair would already be dead.'

'Why does Moran seek Li so doggedly, if not for revenge?'

'Ah, there you touch upon the mystery. Li has sought advice and assistance from many people during his return to this country, and to a man, each one has been murdered by Moran. What's more, they are being tortured for their information on Li's movements. Moran is covering his tracks, and is relentless.'

'Have you any theories?'

'Wild fancies only, thus far. I have no data, save that Moran pursues Li with savage determination. But today we meet the first of those unfortunate souls to survive the interrogation. He may be able to shed light upon this terrible business. He's one of the few who is not a Chinaman, as well, and therefore may have more intimate ties to Li and his Australian origins.'

'Who is he, then?'

'His name is Alistair McLeod. He's a Scotsman, although born here in the colony. He and his Chinese wife were leaving the theatre two nights ago when they were accosted by a man I believe to be Colonel Sebastian Moran. Witnesses say that as Mr McLeod was manhandled into a carriage, he cried out to his wife to flee, which she did, but she has since made no statement to the police. She's said to have taken to her bed with fever. She will not take visitors, nor leave to visit her stricken husband.

'Mr McLeod was found stumbling through the streets late yesterday afternoon – he nearly fell into one of those open drains before a policeman escorted him to hospital, where he lies in a fevered wrack of fear. The poor fellow bears the same strange and terrible wounds as many of Moran's other victims. It is those upon which I wish to have your advice, as well as any insight you may have into his ravings.'

The two men had come to a row of terrace houses. A sign proclaimed the two conjoined buildings on the right to be a part of St Patrick's School, but the board on the left-most of the terraces stated that it was soon to open as St Vincent's Hospital, founded by the Sisters of Charity.

'The current hospital is in a cottage behind these buildings,' explained Holmes, leading the way, 'It's normally an outpatient clinic, but as McLeod and his wife had been valued fundraisers towards the hospital, the nuns agreed to care for him until other arrangements can be made for his care.'

The cottage was surrounded by trees and shrubs that affected an air of privacy and comforting homeliness, as well as reducing the summer heat for the unfortunates who waited in a front parlour for their appointment with the Sisters. Holmes approached a closed door at the end of the passage and rapped on it lightly. A young woman dressed in religious habit opened it, her expression harried and her pale face flushed with exertion.

'Sister Wright,' said Holmes, 'I have brought the specialist for Mr McLeod.'

'Oh, yes,' said the Sister, hurrying out of the way, 'Down the hall, then. I'm sorry, I must get back to Mrs Farrer and her baby.'

'You told them I was a *specialist*?' hissed Watson as he and Holmes stepped down the hall to the room from whence they could hear sounds of distress.

'We *are* specialists,' said Holmes shortly, 'Although not in any medical field. Yet I fancy we'll be of more assistance to McLeod, and to any of Moran's victims who come after him, than any nerve specialist.'

Watson held his tongue and they entered the sick room.

The room contained two beds, one of which was empty. In the other lay the poor Scotsman, tied to the bed in an attempt to keep him from self harm as he writhed and whimpered on the sweat-damp mattress. The sour smell of fear intermingled with that of sweat and carbolic in the little room.

Watson examined the chart on the table before handing it to Holmes and placing a hand on the fevered brow of the patient.

'Mr McLeod, my name is Doctor Watson. I'm here to help you.'

The man's eyes opened, bulging out of his sockets in a grim spectacle of a man gripped by terror. 'Is he safe? He hasn't come. Why hasn't he come? For God's sake, tell me he's not hurt!'

'He's fine,' said Watson soothingly, without any idea of who "he" might be. McLeod subsided into weeping. Watson withdrew his pocket watch, took the man's pulse and then bent to examine the strange and dreadful injuries on his face, throat and upper chest. Small scratches around his ears and forehead indicated where the man had scratched and tore at his own skin in paroxysms of distress, necessitating his restraints. The other injuries were more horrible still.

Shallow strips of flesh had been cut out of the skin, long and slender as a bootlace, in four locations. One began at the man's jaw and ended at the lobe of his left ear. The skin was inflamed, though Watson was relieved to note the wounds had been properly cleaned and treated. They were not infected, and not even particularly dangerous to the patient. They'd have been horrible to endure, but hardly explained the patient's prostration of brain fever and terror. Watson brought out his stethoscope and other tools of his trade. He checked the dilation of McLeod's eyes and listened to his heart.

All the time Watson carried out his medical duties, Holmes examined the ruined man from head to foot. He spent some time studying his clothes and feet, and a tattoo the man bore upon his lower arm.

'Can you tell me what happened, Mr McLeod?' asked Watson in his most soothing tone.

'It gnaws in my ear!' The sudden cry descended into a shattered groan of despair. Alarmed, Watson inspected the man's ears again, but apart from a small scrape near the entrance to the ear canal of the left, he appeared unharmed.

'I can see nothing in either ear, Mr McLeod.'

'Get it out! Get it out! The red leech! Get it out!' cried McLeod. His hands strained against his restraints towards his head.

Holmes's head whipped up at the phrase. Then, thoughtful, he took to the patient's cupboard to examine its contents.

Watson could find no blockage in the man's ears, and so relied upon his bedside manner and a few soothing tricks. He took his tweezers, making sure that his patient saw him do so.

'I'll remove the leech, Mr McLeod, but you must remain very still.'

McLeod stared at him, goggle-eyed and panting. 'I feel it in my skull. I-I h-hear it. Oh dear god, I hear it eating at me.' He moaned and began to sob.

'Hush, now,' soothed Watson. He carefully made a show of examining the ear that carried the abrasions. They didn't go deep, but might of themselves leave lingering sensations.

Careful not to place the tweezers too far down, nor to touch the walls of the canal, Watson pretended great concentration and then conducted a subtle performance to indicate some small thing had been removed. 'Hold still!' he remonstrated when McLeod tried to turn his head.

'Let me see it! Let me see it!'

'With your fussing, I have dropped it,' said Watson with just the right touch of crossness, 'But I assure you, it's gone.'

McLeod lay on the bed, panting, weeping and staring at Watson in anguish.

'I hear it!'

'The thing has done some damage to your ear canal, leaving a ghost sensation. But it is gone, I promise you.'

McLeod sobbed. 'My Ling, my Lily. Is he safe? The blackguard didn't hurt my Lily?'

'Your wife is well and at home, Mr McLeod,' said Holmes quietly over Watson's shoulder, for as far as he knew she was, 'But who else is it you fear for?'

'June. The wretch. It's all her fault.' McLeod bucked against the restrains. 'Oh, oh god, it's there. I can feel it.'

Whereupon the poor man began to buck and weep and rave, losing what little reason he had to delirium once more. Watson went to the door for a nurse to order further sedatives. 'When he is lucid,' he instructed, 'Reassure him that his wife is well. I fear we may do nothing for him but provide reassurance and rest.'

'We knew that,' said the nurse, tersely, 'I don't know why we needed a specialist.' She stalked off to obtain the laudanum.

As soon as Watson had packed up his medical bag, Holmes marched him out into the garden.

'What do you make of his injuries, Watson?'

'He appears to have been very deliberately cut with a knife, though why such strange strips should be cut from him, I fail to understand. The cuts are shallow and won't cause permanent injury, and thus far infection has been avoided.' Watson pulled on the end of his moustache. 'The man was insensible with fear, yet the cuts are so meaningless – not deep enough to threaten life and although painful, not agonising as deep wounds can be. It's difficult to imagine how they are connected to his mental state, although they must be.'

'Such wounds have heralded the death of four men in this continent alone.' At Watson's surprise, Holmes continued, 'After enduring peculiar torture with such cuts, each of the others died, of fear in at least two instances. I was not able to examine all the bodies.'

'Mr McLeod's insistence that something…'

'A red leech.'

'…a leech was in his ear was unfounded. I found no trace of such an awful thing, although his ear was abraded. I'd say that a knife with a blade of around an inch in width was held to his outer ear and twisted, from the marks on either side of the anthelix and fossa triangularis, and the small circular cut on the cavum conchair, where the tip would have rested.'

'Exactly, Watson. And why should Moran have done such a thing?'

'From Mr McLeod's hysterical state, I can only imagine that someone wished to convince him that a leech was in fact entering his skull in that fashion.'

'Yes.' Holmes was thoughtful. 'We must suppose that he's used the same method with others to extract information on Li Ju-Long's movements – I was not able to make a close inspection of all the victims, beyond confirming the same strange wounds.'

'Surely nothing would keep you from discovering all you could.' Watson's tone hovered curiously between bitterness and the admiration of old.

'Well, it was hardly politic to argue the point with a crocodile on one occasion, or a pit of fighting dogs on another.'

'Oh.' Watson contemplated the matter. 'Moran is a vicious devil. McLeod's lucky to have survived the encounter.'

'Luck or his own brute strength, Watson. The report of his admission to the Sisters of Charity which I rooted out before your arrival indicates he was found babbling in the street. He's a strong fellow. I imagine he broke free of his captor and was found before Moran could regain him.'

'This is a cruel business, Holmes. Men tortured to death to find the Chinese lad. I hate to think what Moran will do when he catches up with him.'

'Then it's up to us to prevent it.' Holmes clapped his hands together with decisive enthusiasm. 'But let us first pay a visit to Mrs Lily McLeod. She was there when her husband was abducted and may be able to provide some further insight.'

'And explain this reference to June, and the "he" that McLeod is so worried about.'

'Indeed, Watson, there are too many unknown characters in this murky drama.'

'Could "June" refer to the month?'

'No, no, Watson, he gave us that name in direct response to a question about the "he"' for whom he feared.'

'Yes, but June is a woman's name.'

'Exactly. I'd suspect he had misspoken Li Ju-long's name, except that he said "it's her fault". His pronouns are at sixes and sevens. General confusion may be associated with delirium of this kind, but surely not so specific a linguistic disorder. Unless you know of any such cases.'

'None,' Watson had to concede. 'And on such short examination, I cannot even diagnose the reason for his condition, apart from the fact he must have been frightened out of his wits. There is no indication that anything entered his ear canal – the abrasions are external. He may recover from the breakdown in due course, if he has sufficient rest. I wonder that his wife doesn't visit him. It would do much to reassure him that she is unharmed.'

'We'll ask her about it,' determined Holmes.

'What did *you* learn from the visit?'

'You know my methods, my dear Watson!' began Holmes cheerfully, but his dear Watson bent a sour look upon him. He sobered at once. He pressed his thin lips together, then continued, a blank expression upon his face.

'Mr McLeod lives on the outskirts of Melbourne now, but developed his considerable fortunes upon the goldfields. He spent some time among the Chinese miners there – he has an unusual tattoo of a dragon entwined with a rabbit, both in the Chinese style with the delicate colouring typical of those markings. He was not robbed, despite the obvious signs of his wealth – his pockets contained a valuable watch and over thirty pounds in coin and notes. He carries a piece of quartz liberally veined with gold attached to a set of keys which he kept in his other pocket, a good luck charm I imagine. His luck has certainly held in these difficult financial times – his hat, collars and coat were new, did you see? His business interests in Melbourne reside in tea houses and textiles – silks primarily. He's a man of sober habits generally, a non-conformist who lives quietly, though childlessly, with his Chinese wife.'

Watson absolutely refused to be astonished, or to ask how Holmes had reached his conclusions. Holmes's shoulders drooped, but then he squared them and led the way into Victoria Parade.

'The make-up of his family and character are obvious when you…'

The explanation was never made. Holmes, peering along the street and at the shadowed doors and tower of the fire station opposite in habitual caution, suddenly tackled Watson about his shoulders and they both crashed to the path, Watson taking the brunt of it as Holmes fell on top of him. Watson's shout of protest as was aborted by the crack of gunfire. He pressed his face against Holmes's chest to avoid the spray of stone chips that flew out from the brick fence beside them, at the same time reaching up to wrap his hands around Holmes's skull, the only protection he could immediately offer. Another bullet flew closer, and Watson found himself unable to escape from under Holmes's wiry strength, pinning him to the ground.

'Holmes!'

'Keep your head down!'

'He'll get away!' Watson narrowed his eyes up at the tower.

'He's already gone!'

Watson strained his head to see where Holmes was looking – 40 yards away on the far side of Victoria Parade, a man with a rifle darted out of the shadowed arches of the fire station and leapt into an already moving two-seater.

'Moran,' observed Holmes with a scowl. He rose at last, and in a moment was at the brick fence with his eyeglass and pocket knife. With a *Ha!* of triumph, he pried a flattened bullet from the stone and dropped it into his pocket.

Watson frowned at what seemed to him the remnants of a soft-nosed revolver bullet, though fired from a rifle of some sort, and was arrested by the blood spattered across Holmes's cheek. 'Holmes!' he cried, more worried than angry this time, and raised his hand to check the wound.

Holmes jerked away from him and smeared his fingers through the blood. 'A scratch, old fellow. Nothing to signify at all. Come along. I'd hate for Colonel Moran to reach Mrs McLeod before we do.'

Holmes was already waving down a hansom as Watson regained his feet and his medical bag, and tried not to contemplate with horror how he'd very nearly lost Holmes again mere hours after he had found him once more.

Chapter Seven

The well-appointed little Brunswick home, facing Royal Park on the north side of Park Street, appeared undisturbed when Holmes and Watson reached it. The curtains were drawn, upstairs and down in the bay windows on the left, and in the shadowed recesses of both balcony and ground floor. Elegantly-wrought iron lace decorated the eaves and the balcony with floral motifs, and a lamp stood by the gate. The front garden was small and orderly, with artfully arranged white stones and large glazed pots of plants.

Holmes had dabbed the blood from his cheek during the drive, and was as impeccable as ever as he knocked on the crimson-painted door. No reply came.

'Perhaps she's fled?' suggested Watson.

'The curtains in the upstairs room moved as we arrived. A servant would have answered the door. I've no doubt that it's the lady of the house.' Holmes knocked again, then knelt to listen at the mail slot before speaking through the narrow gap. He spoke in what Watson knew to be a Chinese dialect, though which one he couldn't say. He recognised Holmes's own name in his words. Watson inspected the street, but it remained empty, as did the park beyond.

A frail voice replied in the same language. Holmes responded, voice gentle, then rose to his feet.

'I have told her we have news of her husband, and of their enemy, and that we're here to help.'

'I didn't know you spoke any of the Chinese dialects.'

'Oh, I've spent some time in Tibet and China. It seemed useful to learn Cantonese and some Mandarin.'

The door opened a fraction and they saw a pair of frightened eyes peering out of the darkened hallway.

'Does my darling live, Mr Holmes?' Mrs McLeod's voice was husky with tears and anxiety.

'Your husband lives, madam, and with care will make a full recovery, I'm sure,' replied Watson kindly

'And that evil man?'

'We have every intention of apprehending him,' said Holmes, 'But we need to speak with you, and this is not is the safest place for such a discussion.'

Mrs McLeod hesitated and then, remaining partly hidden by the door, she opened it sufficiently for the two men to enter. She pushed it hurriedly shut behind them and locked it.

Mrs McLeod was petite and slender as a reed. Watson thought in ordinary circumstances her presentation was refined. Now, however, she wore an ill-matched hat with the veil hastily tugged down to cover her face.

'I'm so sorry,' she said nervously, 'But I- I'm so afraid. Alistair is well, you say?'

'Not *well*, Mrs McLeod, but alive,' said Watson. 'He'll fare much better once he is assured of your own good health.'

Mrs McLeod placed a hand over her veiled face and breathed a shuddering sigh. 'If only I dared.'

Holmes peered at her ungloved hand with interest, then at her tense jaw.

'Let us repair to your parlour, or the kitchen at least,' he said matter-of-factly, 'If the maid has gone, then the good Doctor Watson will make you a pot of tea.'

Mrs McLeod hesitated before gesturing down the hall towards the back of her home. They came to a small parlour, though with the curtains drawn the room was dim and stuffy. Mrs McLeod immediately sat on the chaise longue which put her back to the window.

'It's all right, you know,' said Holmes as gently as he could, displaying that great kindness he could show to deeply troubled clients, 'Your secret is safe with us, Lily. You may speak frankly.'

Lily's hands clenched convulsively in her lap. 'I don't know what you mean, Mr Holmes.'

Nor did Watson for a moment, but he belatedly looked where Holmes had earlier scrutinised – towards the woman's hands and then towards her face in the low light, and understood.

Faint stubble and a small cut, missed in too-anxious ablutions, marked the underside of Lily McLeod's jaw. Her hands were less feminine than expected, bearing fine, dark hairs along the back of them. Watson could see the slight bump of an Adam's apple at her throat, which the high collar of the dress, askew with haste and distress, no longer covered.

Instantly he thought of poor, ill-fated Wilek – Polish rather than Chinese, but similar in their slender grace, their lovely eyes, their delicate bone structure. Henry had loved Wil so very much, and it had brought ruin to them both.

'How long have you been... married, Mrs McLeod?' he asked.

She darted her ever-more frightened eyes towards him. 'Almost twenty years.'

'Then may you have as long again with him,' said Watson, 'I wouldn't for the world denounce you, and you may be certain that Mr Holmes is a man of his word. Your secret is safe, only you must be calmer and take more care. We can see where your hands shook as you shaved this morning – you have missed a patch and cut yourself. I assume you usually wear gloves when you have company.'

'You must tell us everything you know,' said Holmes, more sternly, 'If we're to stop the man who hurt your husband, we must know it all. To begin with, does he know about you?'

Their client raised trembling hands to the hat and removed it and veil both. Looking at them now was a man near their own age, delicate of bone and with a youthful prettiness, though his eyes were red with crying.

'I don't think so. When Alistair told me to run, I did. I fled. Like a coward.' The man covered his face with his hands and wept. 'I'm so ashamed.'

'Your husband was abducted by a very violent and accomplished villain, Mr... Mrs...'

He raised his chin. 'My name is Li Ling. Alistair and I met in the goldfields and we... we fell in love. When he made his fortune and left, I left with him disguised as a girl. We have lived as husband and wife ever since. He calls me Lily, but in our private moments, I am still Ling to him.'

'Ling, you could not have kept Alistair safe, and your secret would surely have been exposed if you'd tried.' Watson patted Ling's shoulder soothingly.

Ling nodded. 'This man, I heard him shout at Alistair. He said, "You'll tell me where he is or you'll suffer for it".'

'Your husband was attacked by one Colonel Moran. Moran has been hunting for this man Li for months, while I've been, I'm afraid, too many steps behind. Why would he think your husband knows where Li is.'

Ling's face creased in horror. 'Li, you say? Who is Li?'

'Li Ju-Long was a junior member of a terrible gang of criminals. He has betrayed them and fled here to Australia, where he has family.'

Ling pressed his small hand to his mouth and his eyes grew wider in alarm and distress. 'Oh. Oh no. We must tell Wen and Mary at once, and James too.'

Holmes reached towards Ling eagerly. 'Why?'

'We thought Ju-Long was dead,' Ling explained, his voice shaking, 'He became entangled with a gang, led astray by his rich English friend, and left his family to run wild in Melbourne. He went home to his family one last time five years ago – we thought he'd returned to make amends, but he hadn't. He left again immediately. Soon after, his father, Li Wen, fell ill. Mary had to care for him, so Ju-Long's sister went after him to persuade him to undo what he'd done. Days later a terrible brawl was reported in the opium den where we knew Ju-Long worked for this English gang. Many people were killed, some Europeans and more than a dozen of my countrymen, though a fire in the den meant that many were not accounted for. Neither Ju-Long nor Jun were heard of again and Ju-Long's friend left the country shortly afterwards. We had thought them both dead. Now this man is seeking Ju-Long, you say? My nephew lives?'

'Your niece may have died in the fire while seeking her brother, but your nephew made his escape to England with his friend and continued his gang activities there. That gang has broken up and now he's on his way home.'

Ling shook his head. 'I don't know whether this news will bring joy to Wen or break his heart completely.'

'I perceive that you are Li Wen's brother, and the Mary you spoke of is his wife?'

'Yes.'

'And James?'

'James Crosby is Mary's brother. He and Alistair are old friends.'

'Where is Li Wen now?'

'Wen never recovered his health after his children died, and three years ago moved to Bendigo. He hasn't improved. Mary sent word last month that they are returning to Ararat to keep house for her brother. James manages the bank in Ararat.'

'This news was known to your... husband?'

'Yes. Is it important?'

'I have no doubt that Moran elicited this information during the course of his encounter with Mr McLeod. The greater question is, did Ju-Long ever know of his parents' move to Bendigo and does he believe they reside there still? Even if he does, is the family home his destination? There's more to his abrupt departure than you're saying, Ling.'

Ling would not meet his eyes.

'I can't help you or your family if you fail to disclose all the facts to me!' Holmes's voice rang throughout the darkened room.

'It was a matter of much shame to Wen, and the whole family,' confessed Ling reluctantly.

'What did Ju-Long take that broke his father's heart and sent his *sister* into an opium den to get it back?'

Ling wrung his hands and then curled them into fists. 'A puzzle ball from Sun Ning,' he said softly, 'The White Dragon and Jade Phoenix: a puzzle within a puzzle, the first of white marble, the second of green jade. Once opened, it contained scrolls so small they could be held in the palm of the hand.'

'Valuable?'

'To a collector, possibly, but moreso to the family. We spoke of it as our Great Treasure. I believe that Ju-Long thought it of much greater value, that it contained gold. When he took it, Wen could not believe it and accused others of the crime. Soon the whole community knew that Wen had lost control of his son.'

'Where do we find James Crosby?' demanded Holmes, his considerate gentleness vanished under urgency.

'Bell Street, in Ararat.'

Holmes sprang to his feet. 'Watson, come, we must start for Ararat immediately.'

Watson drew a silver cigarette case from his pocket, and took a calling card and a small stub of pencil from it. He wrote his Collins Street lodgings on the reverse of the card and handed it to Ling.

'While we're investigating, if you feel unsafe here, I'll leave word with my landlady that you, with or without Mr McLeod, may use the room. In the meantime, can you take a trusted servant with you to see him? I am certain it will do much to restore him to know that you are safe. He asks after you and is afraid for your safety.'

Ling, blinking away tears, took the card. 'I sent the servants away, but our coachman, Danvers, is staunch. He doesn't know my secret, but he's a good man.'

'Then have him escort you to the hospital. If you can see Mr McLeod and sit with him, it will make all the difference, I'm sure. His physical injuries are not so bad.'

Watson joined Holmes on the street, his bag in one hand, cigarette case in the other. Holmes's fine, thin lips were twitching in a melancholy smile and his mind seemed very far away.

'Well?' asked Watson frostily.

'Well,' said Holmes, rousing with robust cheer, 'You'll come with me to Ararat?'

'I'll see this case through, as I agreed.'

'Ah, yes.'

'Should we not be following Moran rather than the lad?'

'I'm very weary of being five steps behind our quarry, Watson. It's better we run *his* quarry to earth, and then lie in wait for him to appear. '

The notion contained good sense, Watson decided, as he tucked the cigarette case back into his inside pocket. From the corner of his eye, he saw Holmes's small, sad smile.

Oh, realised Watson. *The cigarette case. His cigarette case, which he left for me at Reichenbach.* It still contained the letter Holmes had written him, much re-read over the years, every time filling him with the same tumble of despair, fondness, anger and the most profound sorrow.

'You say the letter was genuine?' he could not help asking.

'Upon my most solemn oath, Watson, it was. I truly thought I was meeting my doom. When I watched you investigate from my ledge, it grieved me to see how affected you were by my perceived demise. I nearly abandoned my hastily constructed plan so that I could reassure you. But I could not. A great deal was at stake, not least of which was your own life.'

Watson patted down his coat, smoothed his moustache and peered up and down the street until he could trust his voice.

'Well, then, we must return to my lodgings for some necessities. Where are you staying?'

'Ah, Watson, I carry on my person all that I currently own, and as the funds I require were only provided by my brother this morning, I have been limited in my options. I've spent several refreshing nights under a tree in the Botanic Gardens. A strange irrigation structure named Guilfoyle's Volcano affords reasonable shelter from the wind and a store of water for simple ablutions.'

'You're not serious!'

'Perfectly serious. The weather is warm. It has been no particular hardship.'

Watson stared at him in annoyed concern as Holmes waved down a cab. 'In that case, I insist that you take one of my fresh collars, at least, and I'll have Mrs Gallagher bring a basin of hot water for you. And we'll eat before we depart, for I doubt you've eaten in days.'

Holmes murmured a negative reply but Watson was not to be moved. 'However angry I am with you,' he said stiffly, 'I did not come all this way and discover you *alive*, for you to continue to neglect your health, as you so obviously have been doing of late. You will bathe, we'll eat and then we'll find a carriage or a train to Ararat.'

Holmes frowned at him, but argued no further as the cab took them back into the city.

Chapter Eight

Watson banished himself from his own quarters, having first laid out some items for Holmes's use – tooth powder, a fresh collar and a spare linen shirt. He sat on the stair, brooding and listening to the faint sounds of trickling water.

He tried not to imagine the scene, but couldn't help himself. It was an old imagining, in any case. Holmes standing in front of the basin in his long, white shirt, sleeves pushed up past the elbows. His drawers draped over the bed, legs and feet bare. Holmes dipping a flannel into the basin of warm water and rubbing it first over his arms, soaping them sparingly, rinsing the pale skin over wiry musculature, before drying his limbs with the provided towel.

He imagined Holmes squeezing the wet flannel so that water flowed freely over long fingers, over his knuckles and the back of his hand, his strong, narrow wrists.

He imagined Holmes washing his skin. Every part of his body. Holmes dipping the wet flannel and then the towel in turn below the neckline of the shirt to wash his neck and upper back. His throat and shoulders and collarbones and armpits. Chest, stomach, hips, thighs. Bending to wash his feet, and to dry them. Again, to wash calves and shins, knees, the curve of his backside, drying as he went, those long-fingered, elegant hands Watson had for so long admired running over Holmes's own body.

He imagined Holmes touching himself in a way that surely Holmes was never wont to do. Sherlock Holmes had made it perfectly clear, long ago, that his body was in service to his mind in all things.

But still Watson imagined. He imagined Holmes's hands lingering over sensitive skin: over the secret strength of his muscles and tendons, over the hair of his chest and the bump of stiffening nub and areole, through the coarser curls at his groin, along the responsive staff.

Watson drew a sudden breath that contained as much anger as horror at himself.

I should not still love him so, or want him so, after the infamous way he treated me.

John Watson had disembarked the *Lenore Ann* only this morning, and here he was, already so undone. Since leaving Baker Street, he'd spent years shunning such thoughts. Back then, aware of Holmes carrying out his ablutions within his room, they were a dangerous yet welcome fantasy, to witness in his mind's eye. To fancy, too, that he might be allowed to… assist. To kiss and touch fair skin, and that such a touch would be welcome, though it wouldn't. Obviously it would not.

After his marriage, away from the stimulus, the indulgence made Watson wretched, as though he were betraying Mary. After losing Holmes, the rare conjuring of the fantasy filled him with such misery and grief that it was more distressing than comforting. He'd firmly repressed it. Until now.

And now his thoughts were once more creating a vision he'd never see, never have, and his body was responding, as it had always done. He was miserable; angry with himself, with Holmes, with Henry who had taught him what his love would cost, and even God, who had given this burden to him.

Watson turned his mind to gruesome battlefield injuries in order to banish such beautiful and forbidden images from his mind, and his prick's eager response to them.

Holmes opened the door, much refreshed. He favoured Watson, who refused to rise from the stair until his body could calm its damned self, with a searching gaze.

'Mrs Gallagher has arranged a light meal for us in the parlour,' said Watson, forcing himself to meet Holmes's eye. 'Then I may pack and we can depart.'

In the parlour, a cold collation awaited but neither Mrs Gallagher nor any servant was there. They helped themselves to luncheon. Holmes was frugal as ever in his repast, though he ate hungrily enough. Watson had lost much of his appetite.

The silence was not the companionable one of old. Holmes kept looking at Watson with dark scrutiny, as though he knew every wicked thought in the doctor's head and was offended by them.

And yet Holmes had offered safety to Li Ling, who dressed as a woman and lived in obvious conjugal congress with another man.

'You were most solicitous of Lily McLeod,' Watson ventured to say, to fill that awful silence with *something*. 'I didn't know your opinions were so liberal.'

Holmes glared at him, sharply disapproving. 'I can't see what harm they do, nor that God should mind it, if it is given to them to love in such a fashion. It's surely inconvenient enough to love in the first place, without society and the law interfering in private business.' Then his tone softened marginally. 'And you, Watson – you have developed a more tolerant stance since my exile.'

Watson bridled at the accusation. 'You have never solicited my opinion on this issue and it remains unchanged. Their liaison is, as you say, their private business which harms no-one. Though the risk they take is considerable.'

'Yes.' Holmes pushed his plate aside. 'Perhaps they find the reward worth the risk. Pack for our journey, Watson. I shall return in half an hour.' He rose, his chair scraping with the speed of his ascent.

Watson rose abruptly with him, blood draining suddenly from his cheeks as a formless panic gripped him. Watson's heart beat so rapidly it rang in his ears. He held his breath, willing the sudden sense of dread and alarm to desist, until his lungs hurt, and his knee ached, and his shoulder hurt, and he thought he might faint.

'Watson? My dear fellow!'

Holmes gripped his elbow as he swayed, anchoring him once more.

'It's nothing,' said Watson, pulling away, glad that his voice was not as tremulous as his pulse. 'My sea legs have not quite adjusted. I do apologise.'

Holmes made to pat his arm but hesitated, hand hovering. 'I will return,' he said softly, 'In no more than an hour.'

'Of course you will,' Watson replied brusquely, 'Why ever would you not?' He swallowed against another surge of panic and made himself calm.

'Very well,' said Holmes, almost gently, 'Be ready to depart when I return.' And he left.

*

Travelling light on short notice was not new to John Watson, though it had been some years since he'd had the necessity. Nevertheless, he had reduced his belongings to a simple bag with a change of clothes, his shaving kit, and, wrapped in oilskin and stowed amidst the clothing for safety, a basic medical kit from the material that had survived the attack on the *Lenora Ann*. One fresh notebook was included, and several pencils. His gun, of course, and ammunition. The remainder of his notebooks and possessions were locked in the trunk.

He descended the stairs to find Holmes had returned, true to his word. Tension uncoiled in Watson at the sight of Holmes at the bottom of the stairs, only to wind tight the moment he began to feel pleased to see him.

Don't get used to him being there, he told himself grimly, *he'll be gone again at his own convenience, as always.*

Mrs Gallagher had let Holmes in, somewhat cross at the day's constant interruptions to her time at the easel. When Watson had informed her he'd be travelling for some days and asked that his room remain undisturbed, she'd been happy enough, since the room was paid for a week in advance. Truly, him travelling was better than having an actual tenant, for it meant the same money at almost no effort.

'My time has been wisely spent, Watson,' said Holmes as he led them to the train station on Spencer Street. 'This morning before your ship docked, I spent time among this city's waifs and found the promise of a sovereign goes as far here as at home towards the gathering of information. It seems that Moran, having lost his chance to eliminate us, has taken the afternoon train to Ararat after all. No doubt he has his own avenues of enquiry.'

'Then we are to go to Ararat?'

'No, we're too late to catch him and if we follow we'll be several steps behind, yet *again*. I've sent a telegram to warn James Crosby of the impending danger, but we can do little else in that direction. No. We need to run Ju-Long to ground – and there I have finally had some better luck. A young Chinese man, recently arrived in Melbourne, has joined a travelling show of riders as a cook.'

'How do you know it's the same man?'

'Because, my dear Watson, I went and had a look at him.'

'You said you hadn't seen him before now – you've been following Moran.'

Holmes gazed at him with fond exasperation. 'I do not need to have seen him before to know that here is a young man of Chinese and European descent but with an Australian accent, who has recently been in Europe, Borneo, down the east coast of Australia and is seeking discreet passage inland, wary of being followed.'

A spark enlivened Watson's eyes. For that second, the old exclamation hovered in his parted lips. But then he pressed them shut on any approbation and he simply nodded. Holmes, on the cheerful verge of explaining in more detail, let go his pent breath and adopted a cool mask.

'The cavalcade has set out for Bendigo, with our quarry among the late-departing workers intending to catch them up along the way by train,' he said brusquely, 'We'll take the next train towards Bendigo and seek him on board, if you are still in this business with me.'

'I've said I am, to the end,' said Watson stiffly, 'You may take me as a man of my word. I don't abandon my comrades in a crisis.'

'You are too bitter, Watson,' said Holmes stiffly, 'And you forget that there are other forms of betrayal.'

'What do you mean?'

'There's our man, now, boarding with the other troupe folk.'

'Holmes, what the devil do you mean...?'

But Holmes had boarded the train. When Watson joined him in the carriage, Holmes's expression was a mask and no further word on the matter could the doctor gain. He abandoned the attempt as hopeless and settled in to ponder the tumult of his emotions. He felt like he was still at sea in that dreadful storm, with an uncertain future at his destination and unseen enemies all around.

The thing seemed a simple matter from here – confront Li Ju-Long on route, learn the full truth of from him and negotiate a solution whereby Colonel Moran might be tricked and trapped. The adventure, and the danger, would be trammelled up in a day or two, no more.

And then, Watson thought, *I will leave Holmes and return to London. There is nothing for me here.*

He longed to take his trunk and walk away from Holmes.

He dreaded both the staying and the leaving, for neither option offered any relief from this heavy pain he carried.

Watson was disturbed in his melancholy brooding more than an hour later by Holmes's frustrated snarl, as he returned to their carriage after walking the length of the train for the fourth time.

'He's not here, Watson,' he scowled, 'I was watching and would have seen him had he left the train at any point. He *must* be here.'

'He must be expecting a pursuer,' said Watson, 'Might he be in disguise?'

'It's unlikely,' Holmes said disparagingly, 'His heritage is difficult to conceal on short notice. I... Oh. Oh, Watson, you shine a light, as ever. A disguise. Of course!'

Watson resented the little arrow of pleasure that shot through him at the praise.

'I'm happy to have been of some assistance, though I'd be glad to know what assistance it actually was.'

'A disguise, Watson. A *disguise*. How has Li Ju-Long kept a step ahead of a great hunter like Sebastian Moran all these months? Through a disguise, that he could take on and off on demand. My own efforts to pin down the man have been futile – in all my enquiries, some days there has been a Chinese man of that name, yet on others, no trace. He's vanished into the air like so much smoke. How could he do so unless by some exceptional disguise?'

'I see that.'

'And do you remember what McLeod said when we spoke with him; the mess he made of his pronouns?'

'That was because Lily...'

'But besides Lily. He said, "June. It was all her fault.".'

'He refers surely to Li Jun, who died in the fire...'

'Who was *said* to have died in the fire. But what proof have we of that? Hearsay. Ju-Long went away to London to join

Ronald Adair? Again, hearsay. Someone joined Adair, certainly, but who is to say it wasn't the sister, who went to demand restitution from her wayward brother and met this dashing Englishman in her brother's company.'

'That is mere speculation.'

'True. Yet speculation meets with the facts as we have them. Li Jun goes to Melbourne to persuade her brother to return the artefact he stole. In the process of this quest, she meets her brother's friend, the Honourable Ronald Adair, and falls naturally into his company. She attempts to enlist his assistance. Li Jun and Li Ju-Long are both at the opium den when the gang fight breaks out. Ju-Long is killed in the ensuing fire and Jun is left to salvage what she can.'

'She follows Ronald Adair,' offered Watson, caught up in the possibilities, 'He must have known she was not the brother with whom he had such an intimate friendship.'

'And must therefore have assisted with the disguise, not only for their departure from Melbourne but for the years following – the linked names Ronald Adair and Li Ju-Long are well known to me among the junior ranks of Moriarty's gang.'

'What sends her back to her family now? Moriarty died years ago. What has kept her away?'

'The treasure her brother stole,' said Holmes, 'It has been no easy matter to retrieve it. Perhaps that was her goal all along. To discover its hiding place and return it to her father.' Holmes took a breath and exhaled. 'Well, it's a working hypothesis. It doesn't explain where Li Jun is now. She was not among the troupe folk when I walked among them fifteen minutes ago.'

'A young Chinese woman alighted at the previous station, Kyneton,' said Watson, brow furrowing as he recalled her. 'I remember, because she was a very comely girl...'

'Well, of course you'd notice a beautiful woman.' Holmes pulled on the chain to stop the train at Malmsbury, next station on the line. 'Come along, then. We must make our way back to Kyneton as swiftly as possible, and hope we're not too late to intercept her.'

'What on earth will she achieve at Kyneton? It's twice as far to Ararat from there as it is to Bendigo.'

With a sudden cry, Holmes leapt from the carriage and dashed down the train to third class, where the other troupe folk were gathered. He returned with colour high in his cheeks and eyes bright.

'Mark me down as a complacent fool, Watson. I have become a blunt instrument during my exile. Her companions say that Jun received a note from the Kyneton stationmaster. She was alarmed at whatever it contained, and told her companions that she'd been followed onto the train by a rough and persistent suitor. She took her bag and departed, stating she intended to go to her uncle, who would protect her.'

'James Crosby.'

'Exactly. We have been spotted and scared her off. Did you see a horse led out from the livestock car at Kyneton?'

'Yes, a very fine chestnut.'

'A strong beast? Good for an endurance ride?'

'It seemed more a flat racer or an animal for the steeplechase...'

'Women and horseflesh, Watson, two of your most reliable vices. She's stolen one of the troupe's horses. Now that

I have discovered its absence, they are raising a ruckus over its loss. Our little bird has flown with the means of her escape. She dare not go to Bendigo now, if she knows we are at her heels. She may assume we know nothing of Ararat, and is now riding there, hoping for sanctuary.'

'But Moran is on his way to Ararat already.'

'Yes. Therefore, we must intercept her before she reaches her destination. Her life may depend on it.'

Watson seized his valise and leapt out of the train alongside Holmes. He stared in disbelief as two scruffy horses were led from the horse car and up to them.

'Holmes. Why are they giving us their horses?'

'Less giving, old chap, and more... selling. It cost me almost every pound I had for horses and riding tack. They're not beautiful, but they're sturdy beasts. It took some negotiating – but I promised to retrieve their trick horse from the thief and return it safely to them. At least we can set out at once. I have hopes we may catch Li Jun before long.'

Regarding the wiry beasts, Watson's hopes were less sure, but there was nothing for it. He bent to his bag and began to bundle up items for stowing in the meagre bedroll and saddlebags. Every step of this journey he took with Holmes, he was stripped of more and more of his belongings. Soon he'd be left with nothing but the shirt on his back and his conflicted heart.

He was not looking forward to the ride across the countryside with Holmes.

Except, of course, for the part of him that was.

His heart was a wretched traitor.

Chapter Nine

Their hopes of catching up with the fugitive within a few hours were dashed by the first sunset, although Holmes claimed he'd never held such hopes in the first place. Nevertheless, they kept on, their horses picking their way across the scrubby landscape as the full moon rose. The bright moonlight cast the world into inky shadows and silver-limned shapes. Tall, pale gumtrees speared into the sky, their fragrance both sharp and soothing in the warm air. Nightbirds called and sometimes in the hunchback shapes of bushes and stones, smaller creatures rustled in the undergrowth.

The sky which always loomed closely overhead in London, too clouded and glowing with the city's own light for stargazing, was here a vast dome, spangled with stars and the occasional flash of a comet. The Southern Cross stood out in the sky, a jewelled kite. Watson had once learned to navigate by that constellation, taught by his brother Henry and an old sailor who had come to the goldfields to seek his fortune.

Holmes, who was seeing these stars for the first time, had of necessity to refer to his compass. Watson stole glances at the silver light painting a rim around Holmes's noble profile and lighting two bright sparks in his eyes, set otherwise in the dark shadow under his brows. He never once caught Holmes looking his way. He wondered if he seemed as ghostly and unreal in this strange light as did Holmes.

Holmes's horse stumbled, righted itself. He with sigh he reined the beast in.

'The horses need rest and I suppose we must, too. We'll have to wait until dawn to resume.' He swung off the animal and guided it to where moonlight rippled on the surface of the river they had been following toward Ararat, on a path from Kyneton that should have intersected with Li Jun's.

'How will we catch her?' grumbled Watson, dismounting. He was fractious and unhappy, yet never once considered abandoning Holmes to the hunt.

'Hers is the faster horse,' Holmes said as he unsaddled the horses and hobbled them by the watercourse, 'But ours have stamina. We'll reach her.'

Watson, charged with the lighting of the fire, didn't reply. The day had been difficult, the silence between them growing more palpably tense with every mile. They spoke only to check directions, or to seek for signs of the stolen horse and its rider.

For his part, Watson was acutely aware of Holmes, riding yards away from him. Too lean, too pale, but beautiful still, like a greyhound, and sharp, like a hawk. Holmes was not handsome as society reckoned it, but to Watson he'd always been captivating. Holmes was never so magnetic as when he was on a case, his strong, severe features animated with purpose.

Watson had stolen looks at him whenever he was sure that Holmes couldn't see him do so. Elegant in the saddle as in all things, those beautiful hands of his firm on the reins, his long thighs taut, his grey eyes bright as he scoured the horizon.

Watson could hardly credit that he'd stepped ashore less than a day ago. Here he was, riding across a landscape he'd never thought to return to, with the man he never dared hope to see again.

111

Don't let that sway you. He left you. He doesn't want you, except as a friend, and even then only when it suits him. You're a fool, John Hamish Watson. The only man who knows that better than you is Sherlock Holmes himself.

Watson moodily left his carefully constructed mound of twigs and dry leaves to investigate the bank of the river. He stomped in the grass and peered carefully about.

'Watson…'

'I'm clearing away the snakes,' said Watson tersely. Sure enough, a few yards away, a dark shape slithered away from the ruckus. 'The blighted things gather at watering places. They are terribly venomous but not on the whole aggressive. If they hear you coming, they leave quickly enough.' He bent to inspect the drier stones by the riverbank.

'I have matches…' Holmes began.

Watson, finding the stone he sought, picked up the piece of quartz and dusted it off. Next, he examined the stirrups of the saddles Holmes had laid aside.

'Watson, a flint is unnecessary, I have…' Holmes took the box of matches from his pocket.

'I know how to use a flint, Holmes,' Watson said through gritted teeth, 'Matches are best saved for when we have greater need of them.'

'You make work for yourself,' responded Holmes, irritated.

'That is surely my business and not yours.'

'It's my business when you go to disassemble my riding tack in search of steel for your stubborn adherence to starting fires with flint sparks.'

'I'm perfectly capable of caring for riding tack, you arrogant...' His teeth snapped shut on a suitable epithet.

'I was not aware you were a *light-horseman*, Watson. I thought I knew all your secrets,' Holmes responded lightly, acidity unmissable.

Watson rose with one fist clenched around the quartz, the other into a fist. 'There are a good many things you don't know about me, Holmes. Even if I were an open book to you and your amazing powers of observation, you have not been here to *observe* me these past years. Do not presume to know my secrets.'

'And here we are again. I have explained my absence. I have apologised for it. I had not taken you for such an unforgiving fellow, but so be it. I have sinned outrageously and must pay for it with your ill temper.' Once more, the light-hearted tone carried acid in it.

Watson's mouth was set hard with fury. 'Don't take that tone with me, Holmes. You led me to believe you had *died*. You sent me away on that path and I returned to find only a letter telling me you had expected to meet your death. And it is revealed that you watched me *weep* for you on that cursed path, with not a care for me – only some excuse that the cruel pretence was necessary for my safety.'

Holmes was bristling, too. 'I left you to your wife and your practice. You hardly had need of *me* in London. You had everything a man could wish for.'

'I mourned for you!' snarled Watson, 'For nearly three years, I have mourned for the man I loved and I...'

He was struck suddenly dumb by his own unguarded words.

And then he scowled, because they were spoken now, with none to hear but the man who did not care, and they didn't matter anymore. None of it could possibly matter anymore, for he was a man without hope.

'You died,' he said, still angry, still heartbroken, 'And took half my soul with you, and it was all for nothing. All that grieving I did, *for nothing.*'

Holmes was not softened. Watson had never thought he would be, though the words Holmes spoke next were a different kind of blow.

'Yes, you *loved* me,' sneered Holmes, 'Against your will. You didn't *want* to. Did you think I couldn't deduce your desire for me? Or how hard you fought against it? Why, when it seemed you would finally declare yourself, you took such fright that you pursued the first woman you saw who seemed likely to have you, and *married her.* '

'And I was right to,' Watson shouted, his voice thick, 'You are repulsed. Disgusted by my feelings.'

'As ever, Doctor Watson, you see nothing and observe less.'

'I understand that you find my feelings ludicrous and offensive. Certainly they counted as less than nothing to you when you *left.*'

'You understand *nothing.* You looked at me with love, and you were filled with self-loathing. You began to feel compelled to act on your unwanted desires, and instead married and moved away from me. When I took the opportunity that was offered to me to disappear, I was attempting to make it easier for you to cleanly choose your *wife*, and save myself the ongoing grief of knowing my inversion would mortify you, as you were mortified *by your own.*'

So much was packed into that angry speech, but Watson fathomed the crux of it.

'Your *own*... mortify *me*?'

'You battled your own instincts with such savage energy, there is no doubt that mine could cause you nothing but revulsion.'

As he realised the import of Holmes's speech, it was as though his very breath was knocked out of him. The rage in him slackened. It was not done with him yet, though a wounded confusion overlaid it now.

'Yes, I fought my nature. I fought....,' he determined to say the words, however Holmes may scathe them, '...wanting you as well as loving you. But I also fought it because you made it clear that yours was not a... romantic nature. Nor, indeed, a... a sexual one. Such advances would have been anathema to you, I believed. But more than that, these... these inversions are *dangerous*. I have seen the cruel consequences of allowing them expression.'

Holmes's raised eyebrow, clearly visible in this silver-and-ink light, was more sardonic and challenging than all the words in the world.

Anger flared, but it was swallowed by dreadful memories.

He thinks I would have been disgusted. He says he has suffered as I have suffered. I didn't see it. And I caused it. Because I was afraid. Dear God, I have been so afraid.

And he began, for the first time in his life, to tell another living soul of his past.

115

'My brother Henry died, as you know, in penury, a broken man.'

Holmes's expression made it clear that the purpose of this digression was lost on him.

'Here in Victoria, Holmes, in a filthy poorhouse, for there was never escaping what he'd done. When we were boys in Ballarat – it was 1868 – he was found with his lover. A Polish boy, Wil. It wasn't the first time Henry's... *preference* had caused the family trouble, but it was the first time we could not escape it. Henry was arrested. He was *flogged,* cruelly. They had to do it over days, Holmes, for to mete the sentence out all at once would have *killed* him. My father insisted that I witness it, for there were rumours that I myself...' Watson took another sharp breath. 'Rumours that were not exactly true, yet not precisely unfounded,' he confessed.

Holmes stared at him.

'And Wil. Poor, dear Wilek. He and Henry loved each other. I used to stand watch for them, so they could make their trysts, except for that day. I was at the little goldfields schoolroom, taking my turn at teaching the younger ones their letters, but Henry and Wil were young and in love and didn't want to wait. They were found naked together. Henry was dragged away to the prison. Wil ran. He was found the next morning, hanging from a tree. They say he killed himself, but – the tree was very high, Holmes. He was a beautiful soul but no climber, and the bruises on his arms were strange – I always feared he'd been aided to his death.'

'Watson...'

'Henry was sentenced to a hundred lashes and ten years in prison. I know for a fact that one of the guards told him in unnecessary detail of Wil's fate, for he wrote to me of it and the paper was stained with his tears. I was sent home to England, forbidden by my father to ever speak of Henry again. Henry never told me what befell him in that prison, but it broke him. He rarely wrote after that except to ask for money. When our father died in Sydney, yet again failing to find his fortune, Henry managed somehow to get his watch. It's a miracle Henry had it in his possession when he died, or that he had a friend to send it to me. You're right. I was thinking of… of daring to speak my heart to you, but the watch arrived. I took it that fate was reminding me of the cost.'

Holmes's expression was almost as stricken as Watson's.

Watson's mouth twitched and his eyes burned with the effort this was taking. 'I would not have brought shame and disgrace upon you for all the world, Holmes. Even had I realised you harboured warmer feelings for me, I saw how Henry was ruined by this love. I could not have borne it if the same happened to you because of me. I'd do anything for you, include repress my nature, so as not to appal you with my attentions, or to risk your good name. To be with you was enough. Torture too, sometimes, but... to be your friend and share those adventures with you was enough. They were always the happiest days of my life. I cared for Mary deeply, but she was… the *friend*. The larger part of my heart was always with you. It is to my shame that I believe she was aware of this, and to her great credit that she did not mind.' Watson's voice shook.

'I didn't know,' said Holmes softly.

'So I had some secrets after all.' Watson's shaky laugh was nothing like a laugh at all. 'Yes. I fought my nature, Holmes. But in fairness to me, you had shown every indication

117

of finding such ties repugnant. I would never have forced myself on you, or risked our friendship. If you had but given me *some* indication...'

His words had the unfortunate effect of filling Holmes once more with simmering ire.

'Well,' Holmes said, lips twisting sardonically, 'We have both been the most remarkable fools, it seems. Had I but known the fault was mine...'

'That is not what I-'

'I could have lived with you at Baker Street, just as we were, even if you didn't want anything further, and been happy. You might one day have overcome your fear to make something else. But no. You had to flee from the prospect of even that much. You wanted to have your cake and to eat it, too. To have your great friend, whom you secretly loved and tried not to love, while you could also be married and be acceptable to the wider world. Mary Morstan was a good woman. I truly tried to wish you both happiness. But there you were, at my every summons, trying to have it all. I missed you. And you never noticed.'

'Holmes...'

'I left because I could not bear it, Watson. Not another day of it, to see you so infrequently. To see you for mere hours and then for you to go home to her. I did not plan my escape at Reichenbach, but the opportunity was a godsend. Envy is a poison that gets in at the roots, Watson, and kills the love it feeds on. I wanted you to be happy but I couldn't bear it that you were happy with someone else. So I left. But apparently, you tell me, it is *my* fault. For failing to tell you something that you didn't want to know, because you were too afraid to know it.'

Watson listened to this speech, wrung with conflicted emotions. Sorrow, shock, anger, defensiveness on Mary's part, and upon his own.

But as Holmes glared at him, pale and forbidding, the hardness of his expression at odds with the grief in his eyes, Watson understood.

Yes. He'd been a coward. He had never been a coward in his life, until this matter. But he loved Sherlock Holmes, and desired him, more than he had desired any woman. Even, God help him, Mary, who had deserved better. But all she got was John Watson, who could never give her his whole heart, because most of it belonged to Sherlock Holmes.

It was time at last, decided Watson, to be brave.

Chapter Ten

'I have been selfish,' Watson began, determined to see this through without wavering, 'And a coward. There *were* signs, I know. You gave me... indications, though I did not trust at the time that they could be more than wishful thinking on my part.' Watson's brow and mouth both puckered in self-directed disappointment. 'No. That is not entirely accurate. In retrospect, I'll admit that I didn't choose to see them. I was so afraid of everything that could go wrong. You seemed unattainable to me, and worse, I feared to bring ruin on us both.'

Watson didn't wonder that Holmes's expression remained neutral. Well, after all, despite Holmes's admission, Watson knew he had, through his own cravenness, caused Holmes grief.

'When I finally had built the courage to declare myself...'

'Henry's watch, which I misread,' said Holmes.

'I'm so sorry, Holmes. I beg that...' his voice caught, 'That you forgive me, for my fear. For my... my self-interest. For denying... us... and accusing...' He struggled to articulate his penitence through the grief closing up his throat, as Holmes looked down his hawk-like nose and remained unmoved. 'Please. Holmes, can you forgive me?'

'And if I forgive you?' asked Holmes coolly. 'What then?'

What then?

After ten years of being too afraid to even want; after three more of grieving for lost love, lost chances, the loss of the happiest part of his life, Provenance had seen fit to gift him this new chance. Doctor John Watson was many things at many times, but he was not an idiot and he was not ungrateful.

Resurrected courage stiffened his spine. He met Holmes's grey eyes unwaveringly.

'Then I am ready to risk it all to be with you, if you'll have me. You will not find me wanting again. I'm yours, heart, body and soul. If you no longer wish... no longer desire... then use me how you will. I'll do whatever I must to make it right with you. My dear Holmes. My dear friend. My...'

His words ran out. He waited, pensive and raw.

Holmes's brow creased in puzzlement, as though he hadn't expected this. Watson, so strangely fragile, his open expression showing fully for the first time the depth of his feelings. His shame and his sorrow. His love.

'The risks remain the same, do they not? The things you fear are still the things that may happen. Prison. Flogging. Disgrace. Death.' Holmes's expression was full of challenge.

'What are they to me, now?' Watson's asked, eyes glistening, silver-washed. 'I thought you dead and my world became a lifeless thing, hardly worth the bread it takes to live one day to the next. I thought I could survive and build a life with Mary, but even had we not lost the babies, that life was a... a substitute. God help me. I cannot bear to lose you a second time. You are alive, dear god, Holmes, *you're alive*, and I will dare anything, risk anything, defy anyone, to never be parted from you again. If... ' Watson swallowed but didn't look away. 'That is, if...'

'My feelings for you have not changed,' said Holmes, firm and cool. 'I have been years teaching myself to not love you, and the lessons have not taken. One whisper that your life was in danger and it was all I could do not to fly straight to your side to protect you. I only did not because it wouldn't have saved you, and that was the sole end worth pursuing. But I brought you to me. Of all the ways I might have chosen to protect you – I chose to bring you to me.'

Watson blinked stupidly, momentarily uncomprehending, but as Holmes's words settled in through his skin, his hands shook, daring to hold onto hope.

'You love me, then. You would not... wouldn't turn from me, if I... if....'

'No. No, John, I would not.'

It was a moment for action, if ever there had been, but Watson couldn't move, only stare in bewildered amazement at Holmes.

'You... would not?'

Holmes's smile was not addled with romance. It was the sardonic one of old, although his eyes were warm indeed.

'I'm not a sentimental man, as you know,' he said, his tone leavened with humour, 'I put such things aside for my work. Yet when I perceived you were seeking matrimony with Mary Morstan, I believe I protested my distrust of emotion too much.'

He didn't elaborate on the concurrent use of the cocaine as a distraction, as it had failed in any case to distract sufficiently from his unhappiness. Once Watson had gone to the marital home, Holmes had mostly given up the vice as useless for its intended purpose.

'But I am not without a heart,' Holmes continued, 'And such a heart as I possess belongs to you, as it has these many years. I am who I am, my dear fellow, and I dare say I will be as infuriating as ever, with my work and my bad habits. But as you say – I am yours, if you will have me.'

Watson's eyes and mouth began to crinkle in a comprehending grin. 'Sherlock.' He said the name as though admiring how the intimacy of it tasted in his mouth. 'I daresay my own bad habits haven't much improved. If you're willing to overlook them in turn, then of course, yes.'

'Well then,' said Sherlock, 'We are agreed.'

'We are.'

They stood a hand-span apart, failing to act on their agreement and honestly neither fully clear on what they had agreed to.

Watson looked from Holmes's hopeful face down to his graceful hands. He took them in his own.

"If you're amenable, I'd very much like to kiss you,' said Watson, his voice a-tremor, 'Unless you dislike the moustache. I could shave it, if you prefer."

"Oh no, my dear fellow. Your moustache is one of the many things I admire about your features. And I... John. John.' He seemed to like the shape of that name on his lips.

'Yes?' A question more breathed than said.

Sherlock Holmes's expression softened. 'John, I have longed to learn how your mouth feels on me, moustache and all."

John Watson tilted his head a very little and pressed his lips gently to Sherlock's. He lingered, eyes open but lids hooded. The blood thrummed through him as Sherlock, just as gently, returned the pressure.

They parted a very little and breathed the warm air from each other's mouths.

They kissed again. This time, John closed his eyes and parted his lips and sought the same, and was obliged, as the great man of logic gave himself over to the sensation of that mouth, the brush of that moustache against his lip and cheek. Sherlock tilted his head to achieve a more agreeable angle and sought John's mouth again, kissing more deeply.

John released Sherlock's hands to place his own against Sherlock's face. He kissed Sherlock's cheek, his jaw, the creases beside his eye, the corner of his mouth, his throat. He held tight to Sherlock's waist, fingers flexing, and breathed his plea into Sherlock's ear.

'Oh, my dear, my dear, my dearest, let me kiss you, let me touch you. Say you will. Tell me that I may, oh please. I have longed so to let you know how I love you. May I, oh, may I?'

'Yes.' Sherlock kissed John with such devoted attention that John was left to groan a sigh into Sherlock's mouth, as though relieved at last from a great burden, a terrible weight. His body shifted almost at once from supplicant to benefactor, holding Sherlock close and demonstrating at last the full extent of the love and desire he had for so long locked away, for fear of rejection, of consequences, of costs too great to bear.

When emotion overcame him, John pressed his forehead to Sherlock's cheek, and he held Sherlock tightly in his arms. 'Sherlock,' he murmured fervently, 'I would do things with you that are forbidden by the laws of man and nature.'

Sherlock pressed his lips to John's temple, astonished and moved by the intensity of emotion transmitted by that sturdy body. He'd always known that fear had held his friend at bay, but had not realised until now the toll that both the love and the fear had taken.

'Splendid,' he said with both levity and certainty, 'I look forward to it.'

John, as Sherlock had hoped, laughed. John nuzzled against Sherlock's cheek, tickling him with his moustache. Sherlock turned into the caress, claiming another kiss.

'I must say, the moustache is everything I had hoped it would be.'

John laughed again and the next kiss was more intense, more passionate, and he began to stroke warm palms down Sherlock's sides.

Sherlock, his whole body tingling, stretched his neck to allow John to follow his desires – which appeared at present to be to worshipfully kiss and lick Sherlock's neck. Sherlock insinuated his hands under coat and waistcoat to rub his thumbs against John's ribs.

'As regards to forbidden acts,' he said, 'I think you'll find that nature is not so strict an arbiter. By my own observations, I see that nature allows for relations more varied than the English law.'

John drew back. Sherlock kissed his frowning brow, then his mouth. 'Do listen, John. I observed a breed of rat in Sumatra during my travels – large even by the standards of London. The male members of the breed's large groups at times engage in sexual acts. I cannot see how this is a sin against God, since animals know nothing of the church. Surely then, it's part of the state of nature, that sometimes such attraction is so. Where beasts may rut, men can love – surely that elevates us from pure nature and closer to God.'

'I value the insight,' John said, the old spark of amusement in his eye, 'But I don't believe the world at large is quite ready for the sentiment.'

'I'll be content if you are. We are men of science. Demonstrably nature has nothing against us. Against this.' Sherlock kissed John again. 'Let us abandon that stricture, at least.'

John agreed to abandon it by pulling Sherlock into another passionate kiss. That is how their dialogue proceeded for a time – with nothing but the soft sounds of their mouths together, the rasping of their breath, surrounded by the ripple of the river and the calls of nightbirds.

Finally, Sherlock said, 'We must rest. We have a long way to go tomorrow.'

'Of course,' said John, but his tight-wound arms did not relinquish Sherlock's waist.

They kissed again.

Sherlock said, 'We only have the horse blankets to sleep on, I'm afraid. My negotiations could only take me so far. At least I was able to include a little food.'

'I've bivouacked in harsher circumstances,' said John gamely, 'Though not for some years. You are accustomed to Melbourne's Botanic Gardens, I hear.'

That made Sherlock laugh, which made John laugh. They broke apart. John saw to a low-banked fire – using the matches – while Sherlock spread the horse blankets side-by-side on the ground a safe distance from the flames, with the saddles at their heads. The hobbled horses grazed by the river, unfazed by developments.

They ate some of the rations they had brought with them, and boiled water over the fire for tea, though they took any opportunity to let their fingers brush against each other. Then, fully clothed, the two men stretched out on the blankets. They lay on their sides, facing each other.

For many minutes they gazed across the darkness into the light of the other's eyes, and smiled – contented, nerve ends buzzing with recent joy. The world had been up-ended and set to rights all in one momentous and yet tiny exchange.

'I'm so glad to be with you, my dear fellow. My dearest.' John's voice faltered and silver light glistened in his brown eyes, 'I'm so glad you're alive.'

Sherlock pressed his fingers to John's lips. He smoothed down John's disarrayed moustache and let his fingers trace a path from lip to shoulder, to elbow, to hand. He wrapped John's hand up in his and raised it to kiss his blunt fingers.

'As am I, and glad to be with you. My… very dear John.'

Slowly, their breaths became synchronised and even, and sleep came. Despite the rough blankets and rougher ground, each rested better than he had in some time.

*

John's eyes fluttered open at the touch on his shoulder. His gaze met Sherlock's, their faces painted in purple shadows. The starry sky was flushed with the violet of the false dawn – piccaninny daylight, some Australians called it. True dawn was an hour away. The fire was cold ash and the air was cool.

John didn't speak – only looked at Sherlock as though he might be some phantasm conjured from longing. Then the phantasm brushed his thumb against John's lower lip. John kissed the pad of it, then the heel of his palm. Sherlock leaned down and their mouths met.

In the next moment their bodies were pressed close, hands in each other's hair to hold and caress, John's thigh between Sherlock's legs, and perforce Sherlock's between his, each of them hard and urgently pressing his hardness against the other. John clutched at Sherlock with one hand between his shoulder blades, his other massaging the curve of his behind, while Sherlock reached between their bodies to first rub his palm over the doctor's chest, then down over the swelling of his prick.

'Holmes. Sherlock…I…'

'We must travel in these clothes, John,' observed Sherlock breathlessly.

John blinked hard against the disappointment. 'Oh.'

Sherlock's eyes crinkled with humour. 'But I suppose we should bathe first. We're near a convenient river, after all.'

'That is true,' agreed John, in as neutral a tone as he could manage with Sherlock's hand on him, 'We do need to bathe. And that r-river is m-most convenie-' Sherlock squeezed him softly. '-aaah.'

With commendable speed, they stripped and waded into the river, there to provide friendly aid in bathing. Sherlock explored John's body with the hands that John so loved, examining the scar of the wound that had brought John into his orbit so many years ago, but with no more or less attention than any other part of him. John likewise explored Sherlock, his palms and fingers cupping and flowing over him, pausing at Sherlock's own many scars, including the newest in his thigh.

'You've been hurt.'

'It's nothing,' Sherlock assured him, 'All of it is nothing now that you are with me again.' He silenced any more questions and stole most of John's breath with the passion of his parted lips and his softly seeking tongue.

Naturally, the bath was soon forgotten. John had spotted an incline on the bank. Soon Sherlock was stretched out on the grass, hardly feeling the twigs and stones on his bare back. John was above him, kissing him while he moved with rolling thrusts against the heat at Sherlock's groin.

Sherlock encouraged him, hands on John's buttocks, with soft chants of *yes, John, yes*, and startled moans of pleasure, until with a startled moan of his own, John spent himself. He sagged, panting for breath and kissing Sherlock's chest over and over.

Then, with a wicked, happy grin, John wriggled down and took Sherlock, stiff and hot, in his mouth. His moustache tickled Sherlock in a most stimulating fashion, but that was not nearly as stimulating as John's tongue and lips, and climax soon took him.

John pillowed his cheek on Sherlock's stomach, which heaved with the breathless aftershocks of passion. When the motion ceased, he kissed the pale skin of belly and ribs, over sternum and chest, to Sherlock's throat and jaw, while Sherlock hummed cheerfully.

'Well, John, my dear,' said Sherlock in fond amusement, 'I may hazard a deduction that after you have had your satisfaction, you are a most affectionate fellow.' He resumed his happy humming.

John laughed softly. 'I may hazard a deduction of my own, that you are a most musical one after your own satisfaction. Sarasate, isn't it? No, don't stop. I've missed your music. I long to hear you play again.'

Teasingly, Sherlock feathered his hands over John's shoulders. 'Sarasate, yes. *Romanza Andaluza*. I'm out of practice I fear, although you made lovely music under my hands. The crescendo was most pleasing."

'You may play me as often as you like.' John's tone was smug, 'But I believe we must be on our way.'

'Indeed we must.'

They bathed quickly and efficiently with the bar of carbolic soap from John's kit, John helping Sherlock to rinse twigs and leaves from his back and the fringes of his hair. They ate frugally and filled their canteens. A spare shirt of John's served to dry them, which he lay across his saddle to dry in the sun as they set off towards Ararat, true dawn breaking in pinks and oranges across the horizon.

Chapter Eleven

Two hours later, John shifted gingerly in the saddle, the second day of unaccustomed horse-riding making itself felt. He watched Sherlock sitting tall and easily on his rangy mount, as though this mode of transport were a daily occurrence for him. Perhaps it was, or had been. They had not spoken much yet of their time apart.

Their morning's journey had been slow to begin with, the light too uncertain to take the horses any faster than a brisk walk. At one stage, they'd seen a small group of native men in the distance, spears carried easily over shoulders or loosely by their sides, as they headed out to hunt, for kangaroo, probably.

John wondered if he might attempt to shoot a kangaroo, and whether they'd have time to gut and cook at least part of it, before accepting that they wouldn't. Best to think of something other than food.

He thought of their morning by the river, and then, not for the first time, that he ought to think of something other than Sherlock's body beneath his, or Sherlock's voice crying out in passion.

The case, then.

The events that brought this young woman, Li Jun, to lead them this chase across Victoria were unclear to him, beyond her links with Ronald Adair and Moriarty's wretched gang of enterprising villains. Sherlock would share his thoughts all in good time, which was Sherlock's way. John's way was to allow him undisturbed silence in which to contemplate the many puzzling aspects of the business.

John looked at Sherlock again – his posture in the saddle, the stretch of cloth across his thighs as he sat astride the horse, his hands on the reins. John admired Sherlock's elegant, long fingers (and thought of them on his own back, and his shoulders, his face and throat, his…)

'We passed her campsite fifteen minutes ago,' said Sherlock suddenly, amusement colouring the announcement.

'Did we?'

'You were rather caught up in reviewing other events of the day.'

John attempted to appear nonchalant. 'One needs to do something to pass the time.'

Sherlock was in the mood to indulge him. 'True. The Australian landscape doesn't offer much for distraction. It's the same for long stretches. Too much sky, too flat for too far, unless it's too much mountain, or too much forest, or too much shoreline, and colours as drab as the sun can make them for as far as the eye can see.'

'You're too harsh,' John said, drawing up alongside him, 'The land is made on a very grand scale, but it has sense of boundless majesty about it, don't you think? Nothing in England or the Orient is quite like it – the great dome of the sky is all parched and pale blue now, but I've seen it vivid blue and full of cockatoos with yellow crests, and great flocks of little bright budgerigars. And these gum trees stand like ghosts, but the scent of them is marvellous. It reminds me of nights Henry and I spent in scrubland hunting wallabies and possums for our supper. It's drab on the surface, but see there? All those tiny wildflowers are so much Italian confetti, and there, the green parakeets flying along the river. It's not as lush as the forests of England, but it

132

has its beauties, and I believe I have good reason to think well of the land hereabouts, don't you?'

John arched an eyebrow at Sherlock, to be greeted with a gentle smirk.

'Do continue, John. You have a gift for describing landscapes that I, literary amateur that I am, cannot hope to emulate.'

'Ass,' John declared affectionately.

'I encountered your earlier tales in *The Strand Magazine* during my travels, John, and really, they were remarkably educational in how far one can bend the truth and still at the heart of it not be a lie.' As he said it, Sherlock's smile dissolved – as John's had so suddenly done. 'John?'

John stared between his horse's flickering ears at the horizon. 'It was all I had of you,' he said quietly, clutching the reins. 'No-one to bury, no grave to pay my respects. I'm not so very good a writer, I suppose, Holmes. But it was all I had to keep you near, and the only thing I had to offer to say goodbye.'

'John.' Sherlock urged his horse along so he could place a hand on John's. 'My dear fellow…'

John released his tight grip and turned one hand up to clasp Sherlock's. 'I'm sorry. I don't mean to be such a melancholy creature.'

'I don't mean to mock your grief, John. I bore enough of my own to ever do such a thing.'

John lifted Sherlock's hand to his lips and kissed it, squeezing the fingers before releasing him. 'I know. It's all right. We've both erred enough and grieved enough, I think.'

'Yes.'

'You'll find I wrote most poetically, if erroneously, about your passing.'

Sherlock regarded John with concern, but on observing the latter's relaxed posture and his eyes crinkling with humour, Sherlock set aside his remorse. All was well – as evidenced by John's impudent smile.

'Truly, it's all right,' said John, 'Besides, you forget, I've seen your own attempts at describing our adventures and I'll save your dignity by sparing you my editor's thoughts upon them. There, by the way, is another man you make happy with your return. He was importuning me to simply make up tales about you, for the sake of his sales figures. Imagine.'

'Nevertheless, with your gift for the descriptive and may I say sensational phrase, you may continue to add to your authorial coffers by writing for one of those *green carnation* journals.'

A bark of laughter escaped his companion. 'I shall never write for one of those torrid publications.'

'Not under your own name, certainly, but I believe "Ormond Sacker" makes a tolerable pseudonym.'

'You are incorrigible, Holmes!'

'I merely offer you an alternative market for your undoubted skills as a storyteller, my dear Watson!'

'You'd have me writing lurid sexual fantasies for a crown, Sherlock!'

'Oh, John, I'm sure we can negotiate for at least ten shillings. And I shall illustrate them for you. I am a more than reasonable draughtsman, after all, and I shall have a model at home to render my work lifelike and appealing to the eye.'

John leaned across the short gap to capture Sherlock's hand. Sherlock rode close so that they could steal a precarious kiss before resuming their journey.

Good humour thus restored, they rode on in companionable silence. They paused near midday to water the horses, refill their canteens and mop cool water over their faces and necks. They also shared a chaste kiss, but they had no time to spare for more pleasurable pursuits. Sherlock checked the map and compass and they continued towards Ararat.

In the mid-afternoon, Sherlock gestured towards the west. John made out the shimmer of movement a few miles away.

'She's not so far ahead of us now. There are signs her mount is tiring,' said Sherlock. 'Come along – we can catch her before noon if we hurry.'

Sherlock urged his mount to an easy canter, John at his side. The grey-green shrubs and ribbon of muddy-blue water flowed by as they closed on their quarry.

*

They saw the bedraggled figure ahead of them as the sun slipped past the zenith, and urged their horses to go faster.

The figure heard them and tried to kick her beast to a gallop, but the animal was weary and fractious in the heat. It bucked and skittered sideways. She clung to its neck for a few of its jagged movements but as it twisted, neighing, beneath her, she finally became unseated and fell to the hard earth with a cry.

By the time John and Sherlock drew near, Li Jun had staggered to her feet. She was attired as a man once more, but her hat had come adrift and her clothing was askew in the heat.

She might have been a delicately boned boy, except that they knew her secret, now.

Jun had drawn a pistol and waved it from one to the other of them, her hand shaking, which was more dangerous than if she'd been calm.

John and Sherlock reined their horses to a halt ten yards away.

'Put the gun away, Miss Li,' Sherlock called to her, sitting serenely in the saddle.

'I will not surrender!' she cried harshly, 'Go to the devil!'

'We are not your enemy,' he said, loudly but calmly.

'Everyone is my enemy,' she countered, 'I can trust no-one.'

John kept his eye on the pistol that jittered between one target and the other. Sherlock indicated the woman's other hand, which she held gingerly at her side. The fingers were bent out of true.

'Miss Li, I'm a doctor,' John said in his best professional voice, 'Let me look to your injuries.'

'Hold still!' she cried, fixing the weapon on him as he began to dismount, switching her aim frantically to Sherlock as he, too, swung carefully out of his saddle.

'We have water,' said John gently, 'Which you and your horse both sorely need. And I can see that you have broken bones in your fall. I can splint your fingers and give you something for the pain.'

'You have come to kill me,' she swore, 'That devil Moran has sent you.'

'We have come precisely to prevent his harming you,' countered Sherlock smoothly. 'We know he has been pursuing you for many weeks…'

'He's been murdering those who helped me,' she said, her voice choking short of a sob. 'My brother's friend, Clarence, helped me in Sydney, and he was murdered. I saw it reported in the paper. I wired for news up north, and those men, too, who gave me shelter for my journey, all dead. He's a *devil*.'

'He is a *man*, albeit a dangerous one,' said Sherlock, 'And we have come to stop him.'

Jun stared, caught between hope and despair. 'You can't help me. No-one can help me.'

Sherlock extended an open hand towards her. 'Let us try, Miss Li. Tell us what happened and how you came to impersonate your brother.'

Jun quivered. She lowered the gun. 'Who are you?'

'My name is Sherlock Holmes,' he said, 'And this…'

'You're dead,' she whispered, wide eyed as though he were indeed a ghost.

'Patently not.'

'You killed Professor Moriarty.'

'In self-defence, yes. That much is true,' he said, with a slight bow.

'If you're Holmes, this must be Doctor Watson.' She stared at John, the gun hanging loose from her fingers.

'I am,' said John, 'Please. Let me tend to your injury.'

Li Jun signalled her assent by succumbing to pain, thirst and fatigue, and folding to her knees.

*

Li Jun came to herself with her head on a folded horse blanket, Sherlock Holmes tipping water against her dry lips while Dr Watson gently held her broken hand in his.

'I have given you something for the pain,' he said, carefully wrapping and putting away the empty morphine bottle, 'Hold still while I splint your fingers and wrist.'

She blinked up at them.

'You must tell us everything.'

'Holmes,' protested John mildly.

'Or rather,' amended Sherlock, 'I'll tell you what I know, while Dr Watson tends to you. You may correct me and complete the missing details. Then we shall continue to Ararat and put an end to this, once and for all.' He gave her another sip of water as he began to tell Jun her own story.

'Your brother, Ju-Long, left Ararat for Melbourne seeking excitement and fell in with an unsavoury crowd, led by Ronald Adair, the wayward and less than honourable son of the Earl of Maynooth, Governor of Victoria. Ronald Adair, I know from my own investigations, was already being groomed for a role in Moriarty's international empire in '88. Your brother fell into that same orbit at around that time. In late '89 he returned to Ararat ostensibly to extend the olive branch, but in fact to steal the White Dragon Puzzle Ball. Your uncle Li Ling told us it was of limited pecuniary value, but of course that is nonsense.'

Jun's dark eyes widened even further in alarm. Sherlock brought a folded bundle into view and her alarm became much more pronounced.

'Gently, Holmes,' said John.

Sherlock unfolded the swathes of silk and then wool away from the object he'd retrieved from her saddlebag. He revealed an intricately carved sphere of white jade. A dragon motif entwined over the latticed shape. Through its carved spaces, a second sphere could be seen, phoenixes etched into the green jade ball cunningly concealed inside the first. Further layers of lattice were visible below that.

Sherlock turned it in his hand, picked it up with his other and held it balanced on his fingertips against the pale sky.

'The White Dragon, Jade Phoenix Puzzle Ball. I'm not familiar with this specific example but I found the form intriguing when I encountered it in my travels in China, and met a master craftsman who made them. This, I believe, is made from a single piece of jade, the outer layer being actually a very pale green. It has, as you can see Watson, many layers of carving and not simply the two that are obvious.'

John placed Jun's splinted and bandaged hand carefully on her diaphragm and examined the layers of carving. 'It's beautiful.'

'Beautiful and precious,' agreed Sherlock. 'Miss Li's brother stole it from their father as a... one may call it tribute for entrée into Moriarty's gang.' He let the ball drop carefully into his palm. 'How it came to be in your family's possession, Miss Li, is one of the many facts I wish to learn, but suffice it to say that I spent a large portion of the last few years in China and Tibet and have some understanding of its value, as an artefact and for its craftsmanship – not to mention the jade itself.'

'My great grandfather made it,' Jun confessed, staring at the delicate ball which Sherlock held so seemingly carelessly, 'For the love of God, don't drop it.'

Sherlock placed the ball onto the squares of wool and silk.

'There are eight layers in all,' said Jun breathlessly, 'My father says that his grandfather, Laquan, made it for a Manchurian prince who died before he could pay for the piece. The prince's brother tried to take it without payment. When my Laquan protested, the brother swore ruin, imprisonment and death would be the price. So my great grandfather fled China for the Americas, and then my father brought it here to Victoria. It's our family heirloom now. Our insurance against poverty. My father used it as surety for loans to establish his business as an apothecary.'

'That is a lot of insurance for an apothecary.'

'This country is not often a friend to the Chinese,' said June stiffly, 'My mother's brother, James Crosby, allows… allowed my father to use it as surety for loans to the community, too, when the white bankers wouldn't make the investment.'

'And your brother stole it.'

'Yes. It would have ruined us, but Uncle James said that as long as no-one else knew it was gone, we'd be safe. But it broke my father's heart, that Ju-Long had become so lost to all honour and decency. While my mother nursed him, I left to find Ju-Long and to bring the White Dragon home.'

'You followed him to Melbourne, where he refused your demands, having already handed the piece over to his friend Ronald Adair. So you went to Adair to plead with him personally.'

'Yes.'

'He refused, of course.'

'Of course. He said that it must be delivered to the vault, now that it had been promised and handed to their gang, or Ju-Long's life was forfeit. But he seemed sympathetic…'

'And so you stayed in Melbourne, hoping to change his mind.'

'Or to steal it back, if I could find where it was hidden. I tried to persuade Ju-Long to help me, to restore our family's security and honour.'

So Li Jun's story unfolded, Sherlock Holmes stating what he knew or had deduced of the affair, Jun correcting and completing details as necessary. Doctor Watson, after tending her wounds, gave her food and more water as he listened. He filled his hat with water for her horse too, accepting with a sigh that the beast's need was greater than his own and that the integrity of the hat was forfeit.

Jun, in her campaign to right the wrong her brother had perpetrated, spent much time with both Ju-Long and Ronald Adair, and soon Adair began to woo her. Jun, wary, allowed herself to be wooed, in the hopes of getting closer to the stolen artefact. Her hopes were unrealised. It became obvious that the heirloom was to be sent back to England, there to be held in a treasury of Moriarty's spoils and either sold or held against a time where the best use could be made of it.

Worse, Adair himself was being sent home by his father, and would be the courier. Ju-Long was not moved by his sister's demands. He was angry that Jun allowed Adair to make love to her, and so usurp his own position.

When four members of a rival gang arrived to make trouble one night at the opium den on Little Lonsdale Street, where Adair and his coterie conducted their business, Ju-Long drew a knife to prove himself the only worthy companion to Adair. He killed a rival ruffian, a savage fracas broke out and death followed for many, including Ju-Long. Jun, frantic for her brother, stood over him as he lay bleeding to death on the filthy floor, and in her turn delivered a fatal wound to one of the attackers. Within minutes, the den was in flames and Adair had hustled Jun away to safety.

As Sherlock had surmised, Adair helped Jun to disguise herself as a man so that she might travel with some safety on the same ship that took him back to England. The year was 1890.

Jun's eyes glistened but she refused to weep as the remainder of her story unfolded. How she became Adair's lover and worked by his side in the gang, disguised as Ju-Long; how she continued to search for the place where the priceless White Dragon had been hidden; how Jun discovered she was carrying Adair's child, and was hidden away by him in small but well-appointed rooms on the south bank beyond Westminster Bridge.

How, as the famous Sherlock Holmes began to close in on Professor Moriarty's organisation, Ronald Adair began to make plans of his own. Adair had contacted Holmes, prepared to provide information in exchange for protection, and his offer had been seized upon most swiftly.

'Ah,' said Sherlock with obvious chagrin, 'I knew he had motivations beyond the money we paid, but we never uncovered who or what he was protecting.

'Do not delude yourself, as I did, that his aim was to protect me and our child,' scowled Jun, 'He knew that I had information about the location of Moriarty's treasury that I had never shared with him. Dressed as a man for much of my time in England, I became adept at disguise and learned to trail both the Professor and his lieutenants without attracting their attention.'

Sherlock said to John: 'Li Ju-Long had a reputation for appearing and disappearing like a ghost – a reputation that makes sense to me now. You would secrete a change of clothing nearby, no doubt, and make your entrances and exits not simply in different clothes but as different *people*.' He fixed Jun with an appraising eye. 'As Li Ju-Long, you had quite a name in the gang as an administrator of poisons.'

'I learned of herbs and medicines from my father, and my reputation was cultivated beyond my crimes,' said Jun defiantly, 'Though I admit I am not innocent. My aim always was the restoration of my family's honour through the return of our fortune. I never knowingly murdered any man, though I played my part in rendering many insensible or talkative enough to spill their secrets.'

John cleaned his instruments as best he could and packed the remains of his medical kit away – very little laudanum, no morphine and no bandages. 'What became of your child?' he asked gently. He knew too well the many ways a babe could too soon take leave of the world.

'I had a son,' she said, regret making her voice distant, 'James Li Adair. He was beautiful. Even Ronald thought so.' She closed her eyes. They were clear and full of anger when she re-opened them. 'Ronald persisted in asking for the location of Moriarty's treasury. I put him off, even during my confinement, when my changed body could no longer be hidden from those who thought of me as Ju-Long. When your plans, Mr Holmes, came to fruition and the gang were captured or had fled, and news came of the Professor's death in Switzerland, still I refused to divulge what I knew – that the vault was in a disused Underground station that had been destroyed by fire over a decade ago. By the time I learned this, my belly showed too much to safely search for the White Dragon, or to travel home if I was able to retrieve it.'

'I had my son and Ronald kept us safe in our rooms, seeing to all our needs. For a while I was content. I had not completed the mission I'd set for myself, but I had my own family now, even though Ronald refused to marry me, or allow we'd ever have a place with his family in Park Lane. But James was enough. He was beautiful and he was enough.' Once more, she was steeped in sorrow. 'And then influenza came to London, and my little boy died. I, too, was close to death, but my ancestors knew my work was unfinished, and spared me.'

Jun swallowed down her grief.

'You finally went to the hiding place and found the White Dragon,' said Sherlock simply, 'And you showed the vault to Ronald Adair.'

'Yes. I had tried to enter the vault myself, but it was cleverly designed. I needed his help to locate and traverse the secret tunnel and the door from the underground station at Earl's Court to where the old station had been sealed up. I found what I had come looking for so many years ago. I left Adair there with the things he prized more greatly.'

'This was near April of this year, was it not?'

'Yes,' Jun confirmed, 'I was preparing to return to Victoria directly, dressed as my brother, when Ronald sent agents to seek me. He decided he was not done with me yet, and thought I had other knowledge to share. I was forced to fly to Europe in disguise, through France and Italy before boarding a ship through the Suez Canal to India.'

'And thence to the Philippines, and on to Borneo before the Port of Darwin,' said Sherlock, 'Yes. Sebastian Moran pursued you in those travels, as I pursued him.'

Jun's eyes widened. 'For so long? I had not known. I first learned he'd found me after I read of Clarence's death, on my arrival in Melbourne.'

'Colonel Moran has been on your trail since he learned of the breach of the vault. I was by chance in Natal when word reached him there, and with it word that Li Ju-Long was the culprit. It seems less of Moriarty's empire was destroyed in our operation than I'd hoped.'

'They had many allies in other organisations. Moran had always been their liaison. He spoke for Moriarty in many places around the world. *Oh!* That he has pursued me so long! How many has he murdered in my wake?'

'How many of them betrayed your passage?' Sherlock countered, 'For each of them allowed Moran to stay on your trail.'

'I paid for assistance, but not for silence,' said Jun darkly, 'Moran killed because he loves to kill. He was always a cold one.'

'But why does Colonel Moran pursue Miss Li with such single-minded purpose? She took only what belonged to her family.'

'Ronald Adair, however, did not,' said Sherlock, 'And has been emptying the coffers to cover his gambling habit, hasn't he?'

'I don't doubt it,' said Jun bitterly, 'He thinks himself safe – that the Professor is dead and that Moran remains in hiding.'

'Instead, Moran has been rebuilding the organisation. His contacts in London informed him of the breach. Given the pursuit, I'm sorry to say, Miss Li, that Ronald Adair himself is the one who told Moran of your flight, though not your true nature. Moran has been seeking Li Ju-Long, and you have evaded him this long, as you evaded me, by your ability to travel as man or woman at will.'

Li Jun was shocked at the revelation, and yet not surprised. 'Ronald Adair loves nobody but Ronald Adair.'

'Indeed,' said Sherlock, 'And as soon as Moran discovered I was still alive, he sent word to Adair to murder my friend – a commission at which he failed, thank God.'

Jun's glance flickered to John, and to her bandaged hand.

'And so we come to the end of our story,' Sherlock continued, 'You come to Melbourne and secretly visit your uncle, Li Ling, who lives as Lily McLeod, having learned of Moran's murder of Clarence in Sydney – don't be surprised, Watson, Ling clearly knew much more than he was saying. Too late, however, for soon after, Moran kidnapped Alistair McLeod – who lives, last we saw, Miss Li, fear not. He knew nothing of your whereabouts, but then Ling sent a wire to intercept you at Kyneton, didn't he? To warn you that Moran was on his way to Ararat, where your parents had returned.'

'Ling swore he'd keep my secret,' whispered Jun, 'As I kept his. He was shocked to find that I lived, but he promised to tell no-one. I meant to warn him, in case Moran came for him and Alistair. I stayed no longer than to do so, and left at once for Bendigo. I only realised how much danger they were in when I received his telegram. I fear I'll be too late. They don't even know I'm alive. And so Ronald Adair betrays and then steals from his masters, puts the blame upon me and I've nothing to show for it but shame and death. If Moran harms my family, I'll return to London and put an end to Ronald Adair.'

'There is one more reason that Moran pursues you,' said Sherlock, reaching for the puzzle ball again. 'The thing you took as recompense for your pains.'

Sherlock retrieved his glass from his pocket and examined the piece. 'You have a probe in your kit, Doctor Watson – if I may have it.' He took it from the doctor and, with delicate precision, layer by layer, he aligned the eight parts of the puzzle ball. Once fully aligned, a cavity in its centre was revealed. From it, a small parcel wrapped in silk dropped onto his hand.

He unfolded the wrappings to reveal a pink diamond, cut on five sides.

'The Hortensia Diamond, one of the French Crown Jewels,' said Sherlock, holding it up to the light of the sunset, 'This is the original, stolen in 1830. The one sent to the Louvre in 1887 is an excellent copy, but a copy all the same. I was engaged to recover the original. I had traced it to Moriarty's network until the scent went cold. Or underground, it seems.'

Jun tried to snatch it from his fingers with her good hand, but he held it away from her.

'It's *mine*,' she snarled, 'I have earned it. I have *paid* for it – with my brother's blood, my own, my son's.'

Sherlock wrapped the sparkling thing up in cloth, placed it back in the puzzle ball and deftly rearranged the layers to conceal the diamond once more.

'Perhaps so,' he said. He stowed the parcel in his saddlebag. 'We may discuss that further once we reach your

147

family in Ararat.' He rose to his feet, leaving John to assist Jun to hers. 'If you're well enough to ride.'

'I'm well enough to *run*,' declared Jun, and indeed she seemed angry enough to manage it.

The three of them were soon mounted – Jun sitting in front of Sherlock on his horse, John leading her weary horse behind his own – and once more riding north-west, towards Ararat and Sebastian Moran.

John, trailing them, regarded Jun's slight frame set before Sherlock's. She held fast to the pommel and gripped the horse's sides with her straddled, trousered legs. It was improper to a high degree and also... he found himself envious. Not that he thought Sherlock was at all interested in the young woman. Sherlock had made it abundantly clear over the years that the charms of women were wasted upon him; and over the last day, just as clear that he preferred John's own charms, such as they were.

The truth was that after so recently becoming acquainted with the sensation of Sherlock's body against his own, John resented Li Jun having any access to that same sensation. He wouldn't be able to lie with Sherlock, not even simply for sleep, while she travelled with them. Now she rode closer to him than John could do, even had they been alone.

Still, Ararat was but a few hours away, and they were in any case engaged on the case. Further, John admonished himself, it was unchivalrous and foolish of him to be so envious, like some new husband overly possessive of every aspect of his bride's person. He was not some green youth with hot blood to go jealously hoarding every touch and breath his love might spend innocently on another in the course of daily life.

Especially when his love was Sherlock Holmes – the most extraordinary person he'd ever known. What need have he of jealousy, when Sherlock had made his choice so unequivocally clear? He had chosen John Watson.

In fact, John considered, Sherlock chose to ride with Jun, which was surely inconvenient and uncomfortable, rather than have her ride with John. Perhaps Sherlock was himself a little jealous, given John's history. What was that comment about John's reliable weaknesses being women and horses? Such possessiveness should have been not only ridiculous but annoying, demonstrating a lack of trust. Yet John found he didn't mind so much as he ought. He found he liked the idea, that Sherlock didn't want John and this woman, however much they clearly had no interest in each other, to be sitting so closely. He found that he was relieved that he didn't have to ride with her, to be aware of her petite form in front of him, when he already ached instead to have his arms around Sherlock again.

Discipline, Watson, he told himself sharply. *We are working. We are* professionals. *We'll have time enough to make up for all our lost time when this is over and we return to Baker Street.*

He sat straighter in his saddle, then caught Sherlock's eye. Sherlock smiled knowingly at him.

He has read my mind, as he always does, the devil, John thought affectionately. He tugged on the brim of his water-ruined hat in salute, and Sherlock's expression was impish in reply.

Chapter Twelve

James Crosby's house was south of Barkly Street, Ararat's main thoroughfare, a fine home of timber and stone, befitting a successful businessman in a prosperous town. Victoria's ubiquitous iron lace decorated the eaves of the veranda and its steep gables were elegant. Stables behind it indicated that Crosby the banker kept a set of horses and a carriage.

The sun was westering, the worst of the heat abating as the travellers rode up the quiet street.

Holmes reined his mount to a halt twenty yards from the house.

'I don't like the sound of it, Watson.'

John drew his firearm from his pocket as Li Jun said, 'I don't understand. There's not a sound to be heard.'

'Exactly,' said Sherlock, 'On foot from here, Watson.'

All three dismounted. Sherlock looped his horse's reins into a nearby shrub, expecting that where one horse stood the others would remain. Jun refused a command – made with a silent gesture – that she stay with the horses, and instead retrieved her own gun. The weapon was steady in her good hand as they crept towards the too-silent house that at this early hour should have betrayed some signs of life from its household.

They stole along the side of the house towards the stables. Sherlock gestured for John to remain concealed by the house and took it on himself to slink, silent as a ghost, to the stable door. He returned with a grim set to his mouth.

'Stableboy and the driver both dead, throats cut,' he said *sotto voce*, 'Two horses and carriage gone, with hostages.'

With a cry of despair, Jun lunged for the stables, but Sherlock caught her by the waist.

'There's nothing to be done for them,' he said, 'We must find who Moran has taken, and where.'

At a signal from Sherlock, John rapped loudly on the rear door of the house. A desperate squeak of sound indicated someone within. John rattled the handle but the door was locked. He crashed his shoulder against it but the mechanism was of solid craftsmanship, so with a shouted warning he shot the lock out of the frame and shoved it open onto the kitchen.

Two women, servants by their attire, lay on the floor, tied with rope and gagged with cloth. They stared at this new intruder with huge, frightened eyes. Near them, a manservant lay insensible, tied hand and foot, blood staining the side of his head. Next to him and equally trussed up was a woman in fine clothes who was very pale, her face bruised.

Jun wrenched herself from Sherlock's grip with a new cry of alarm and despair, and she ran into the house to the woman's side. 'Mama! Mama, wake up! *Mama!*' She plucked the gag from the woman's mouth and scrabbled at the knots at her wrists.

Mrs Li's eyes opened on her daughter, but she seemed to think the girl a dream. 'I am dying, then,' she murmured, 'And will be with my children soon.'

'No, Mama, it's Jun. It's me, Jun. I've come home. I'm sorry I was away so long.' Realising that panic was no help, Jun took a deep breath and now pulled more scientifically at the knots. Her mother's hands came free and Jun massaged them to restore circulation.

'Jun?'

'Yes, Mama. I'm here. Hush now. Hush. I'll take care of you.'

John turned from the butler he'd been tending and said softly to Sherlock, who was freeing the other women, 'I can do nothing for him, Holmes.'

Sherlock took the hands of the older of the women – the cook, a woman nearing thirty, whose eyes were wide and her face pale, though she was in command of her senses – unlike the younger, who sobbed hysterically.

'The man who did this,' said Sherlock urgently, 'Did he indicate where he was taking your master and his brother-in-law?'

'He said he needed a quiet space.' She shuddered; sobbed. Took a deep breath. 'He is a wicked man. An evil man.'

'Yes,' said Sherlock, 'And I'll stop him, if I find him. Can you help us?'

She stared at Jun, who was now kissing and kissing her mother's shocked face. 'Isn't that little June? We thought her dead.'

Sherlock tamped down on impatience, but not well. 'Yes, that is your master's niece. If you can pay attention, we may yet reunite them, and with her father as well, if you can remember anything Colonel Moran said.'

The cook pressed her lips together. 'This... Moran... he said he'd spare Mrs Li in exchange for information.' Her glance flicked towards the dying man whom John had laid out on the floor and tried to make comfortable. 'The master keeps a boat by Green Hill Lake,' she said, voice trembling, 'Mr Crosby and Mr Li said they would both go there with him, if Moran let… let the rest of us live. Mr Garcia tried to stop them from going, but that Moran fellow hit him with the best saucepan.' She sniffled and extended her hand, so that her pinkie finger touched the dying man's hand. 'Mr Garcia is a good and decent man, and he never tolerates high-handed bullies. Can we not send Mr Culver for the doctor, or young Bailey? I don't understand why they haven't come from the stables after seeing to the carriage.' She considered Sherlock's impassive face. 'Oh,' she said, 'Oh, I see. Then I had best go for the doctor myself.'

She tottered to her feet, shook her head to clear it, and bent to the reunited mother and daughter.

Mrs Li lay cradled in her daughter's arms, blinking up at her child in dazed hope.

'Mrs Li,' said the cook, 'I'm going to fetch the doctor and the constable.'

Mrs Li was too addled to make much of it. 'My daughter has come home, Beth. Jun has come home.'

Beth the cook took in Jun's male attire, her tearstained face and the tender way the young woman held her mother.

'So she has,' said Beth, 'She'll look after you until I return. Won't you, Miss?'

Jun shook her head. 'I must go with Mr Holmes and Dr Watson to find the man who did this.'

'The menfolk can do that now,' admonished Beth gently, as the men in question headed for the door.

'They don't know the way to the lake,' countered Jun in a reasonable tone, 'And I do. Ju-Long and I played and fished there when we were young.'

153

'Miss, you mustn't. That man is dangerous.'

'I know what he is, but what he's done here is my fault. Ju-Long and I have brought this on our family. My brother is dead. It's up to me to put an end to it.' Jun patted her mother's face. 'You'll be all right until I return, Mama.'

Mrs Li clutched at her hand. 'Don't leave me, Jun.'

'I'll make an end to it, Mama, I promise. You... girl, what's your name?'

The maid, who had ceased to sob and was nursing the glass of brandy John had given her to soothe her nerves, said, 'I'm Clare, Miss.'

'I'm your master's niece. Will you please see to my mother?'

'Jun!' cried her mother.

But Jun was on her feet and running out the door at John and Sherlock's heels. Beth followed, setting off for other help.

John, Sherlock and Li Jun swung into the saddles of their tired mounts and Jun led the way eastward at a gallop. They rode swiftly through the town, skirting busy Barkly Street and then racing along the clearing beside the railroad tracks until they were forced to slow down or risk their horses' legs and their own necks as they approached the southern tip of the lake.

James Crosby's carriage was resting, horseless, on the shoreline. Sherlock dismounted to check for tracks and Jun, grim-faced, jumped from her horse too. John, gun drawn, scanned the bushland for signs of danger. The fact that the horses had been uncoupled from the carriage meant that Moran was not planning to use it again – and that didn't bode well for his prisoners.

A water fowl squawked, disturbed by the activity. A faint rustling indicated wallabies foraging nearby, but no human sound could be heard, at least until Sherlock said:

'He led the men and the horses this way.'

Jun held her gun in her hand once more, her expression set. 'The townsfolk keep their boats up this way, between the swamp to the north and the deeper waters of the lake.' She put her hand out to Sherlock. 'We must take the White Dragon. I must have something to bargain with, besides my life.'

Wordlessly, Sherlock retrieved the White Dragon in its wrappings and handed it to her. She hugged it to herself with her splinted left hand and gripped the gun with her right.

They picked their cautious way along a trail beside the lake, listening until they could no longer hear birds or animals. Nature had fallen silent and drawn away from something terrible ahead.

And then they heard it: the whimper of terror and pain; one man's cry of *"No, no, have mercy, leave him be!"* and another man's blood-curdling shriek of agony, short and sharp, overlain with the third man, laughing.

It might have ended well, or at least not as badly, if not for the horses' unwitting betrayal.

Li Jun, Sherlock Holmes and John Watson were all old campaigners and even stirred by such horror on the ear, they remained silent as they moved swiftly towards the cries.

But ahead, where Sebastian Moran was torturing one man while another watched helplessly, the two carriage horses were stamping their distress and alarm. One threw back its head and loosed a ringing call across the lake, its companion likewise rearing and snorting and calling – and they received an answering call from a hundred yards away, from the three weary beasts that had been left by the water.

Jun broke cover, gun raised, to be met with a pistol pointed straight at her – at the other end of the barrel, a grinning fiend. Moran held a second pistol on Li Wen, tied against a tree.

Beside him was James Crosby, trussed even more tightly yet writhing as much as his confinement allowed. His hands and legs, waist and chest, were fastened with rope to the trunk of a eucalypt. His head too, with a rope around his throat. A swathe of cloth around his forehead and under his armpit kept his head twisted at an angle so that one ear was almost pressed to his shoulder and his throat and neck stretched taut. A shallow strip of flesh had been sliced from his chin to his cheek – a blood-smeared Bowie knife on the ground beside him showed how it had been made. Blood streaked Crosby's face and throat, and at his exposed ear they saw – *oh dear god.*

A leech, blood red, sinuous and slick, undulated lithely along Crosby's neck, its segmented body stretching and contracting along the strip of flesh that had been laid along his face. One end of the strip had been poked into the cavity of his ear, bloody from a wound made with the tip of a knife. It was towards this the hideous leech made its inexorable way. Crosby sobbed and strained away from the thing but couldn't escape the sensation of its soft, oily skin on his flesh.

'Ju-Long. Here at last,' said the smiling Moran at their horrified silence, 'And Holmes is with you. Come out now, and you Doctor Watson, hands up, or I shall shoot the old Chinaman.'

Reluctantly, John and Sherlock, hands raised, stepped out from the shadows among the trees.

156

'You devil,' Jun spat at Moran, 'What have you done?'

'I was passing the time until you arrived, Ju-Long,' said Moran, 'Your uncle wasn't a very helpful chap and claimed you were dead. I thought your father might be better reasoned with if he could see the consequences of failing to be useful.'

'Jun?' Li Wen's voice was faint and disbelieving. 'Jun, is that you?'

'It's your boy, Ju-Long,' said Moran in a friendly tone, 'Now shut up or I'll shoot him right in front of you.'

Wen fell silent, though beside him Crosby continued to babble and strain against his bonds, which cut across his torso and his throat, purpling his face.

'Let my uncle go!' demanded Jun. She hadn't lowered her pistol, though she dared not fire it, with Moran's guns pointed at her and at her father. Even a haphazard shot could kill or maim one of them.

'He's an interesting subject, your uncle. Very stubborn, quite tough. My old comrade the Professor would've enjoyed him. Taken photographs, even. He was ever such a one for new technology. This leech here, I found a handful like it in Borneo, kept them in a box for the humidity, though they didn't travel well. This is my last one. It eats earthworms where it comes from, huge bloody earthworms. But I've trained this one to have a taste for human meat.' With his eyes on Li Jun, John and Sherlock, he said over his shoulder to Crosby, 'The leech chews down its little treat and keeps on going into your brains. When it's done there, I'll tempt it out again with bits of your liver.'

Crosby's struggled more desperately. The rope tightened on his throat and chest, but he couldn't escape the leech. His

157

face grew livid and purple, his breathing choked, his eyes started out from their sockets, and still he strained ineffectively away from it.

'You're lying,' said John, appalled, 'No leech behaves in this manner.' He started forward but Moran's barrel twitched from Jun to him, to Sherlock, back again. He couldn't risk attack, for someone was sure to be wounded or killed if he tried.

'No leech looks like this 'un does either,' said Moran smugly, 'And here it is.'

'You lie to induce panic in your victims,' said Sherlock severely, 'Half of them died of heart failure before you had a chance to kill them. I've seen the bodies.'

'You're a clever bloody bastard,' observed Moran, his teeth showing as he grinned, 'I'd like to see if you can stay calm with that thing crawling around your ear. Might give it a go, once I'm done with this traitor and have drilled a hole in Doctor Watson's skull. It's not sporting, I'll grant you, but I'll make do with expedient. The Professor would've appreciated the sentiment. Now you,' he turned to Jun, 'I see you have that little trinket with you. It had better contain the jewel you stole from me.'

'The jewel is mine,' snarled Jun, 'You and my brother and that vile Professor of yours owe it to my family.'

'We don't owe you a damned thing,' sneered Moran in return, before what she'd said struck him. 'You *are* Ju-Long,' he asserted.

'Ju-Long died in the opium den and burned in the fire,' said Jun defiantly, 'I am his sister, Jun, and I have waited years to right the wrong he committed. I sold myself to the devil to make it right. You are but the devil's mongrel.' She spat onto his feet.

Moran fired his pistol right between her own, and Li Jun did not flinch.

'It's you all right. Ju-Long. I'd know that bloodless Chinaman anywhere. Only your name is Jun, you say? The *sister*. Well, that explains a lot. We all thought you and Adair were filthy inverts, but you got the job done, so what was it to the Professor and me, eh? And you slid out of that business that this bastard Holmes, here, cooked up for us. You and Adair.' Then his brow knit as further realisations came to him. 'How did you manage that, eh? It wasn't luck, was it? You were warned.'

Jun glared at him. Moran jerked his aim suddenly towards Sherlock, who, having lost the moment to strike, stood down.

'Someone told tales,' said Moran speculatively, 'Holmes, you're a clever bastard all right, but you knew things the Professor said couldn't be deduced. We thought Casper Luckett grassed and saw to him proper before we chased you all the way to Switzerland.'

'Ah. I did wonder what happened to him. Porlock, Watson, as you recall from the beginnings of the Birlstone tragedy.' Sherlock didn't elaborate, however, on who the true traitor to Moriarty's organisation had been.

Li Jun, however, was so filled with venom on being confronted with her enemy and stayed from action, could not keep from speaking at last.

'Luckett was not your traitor, mongrel. Ronald Adair's the one who betrayed your secrets to Sherlock Holmes.'

'Trying to protect you, was he, giving you time to escape?' sneered Moran.

Jun derided the notion with a snort. 'The faithless wretch risked nothing for me, and when my baby died, he didn't care. If you wonder who took the thirteen pieces of silver for Moriarty's vicious hide, it was he – the *Honourable* Ronald Adair.'

Behind Moran, Crosby's gasps gave way to a terrible gurgling cry. Li Wen called his brother-in-law's name in anguish and at that very moment, John's horse broke in upon them, braying a call to the carriage horses and tossing its head, the other two close behind.

At the crux, Jun lifted the White Dragon from where she held it snug against her side and shouted, 'If you want the diamond, *take it*,' and threw it at him.

Moran fired at her, but the flight of the orb in its wrappings fluttered in his sightline and the bullet went a fraction wide. Jun cried out as a gout of blood flew from the furrow in her upper arm, but she was fierce and refused to be undone by a flesh wound. She brought her own weapon to bear, but now Moran feinted and flung himself aside, as a bullet from John Watson's gun whizzed hotly past his ear.

Sherlock dragged John to the ground as Moran fired at them again, the bullet exploding splinters from a tree behind where they had recently stood. Jun dived to the ground, coming up against her uncle's limp body and the bloodied Bowie knife in the grass.

For chaotic seconds, all was crashing gunfire, the whiff of blood and hot metal, the braying of the frantic horses, Li Jun shrieking curses in Chinese and English, and Li Wen calling James's name in grief.

Then, the Bowie knife in her grasp, Jun tucked her feet under her and sprang at Sebastian Moran while her father cried helplessly for her to stop. She brought the knife down in an arc as he raised both pistols, thrusting the blade towards his throat.

Moran twisted, throwing her slight body aside, causing her to lose the knife, but one of his guns also flew free, as did the White Dragon. He turned the movement into a swift roll to his feet and a lunge. He caught at the halter on the carriage horse that was attempting to break its reins free of the branch that held it. He flipped the reins free from entanglement, seized the animal's mane and with a powerful jump, leapt onto its bare back and drummed his heels against its ribs.

The horse, frightened beyond bearing, took off, with Moran clinging to its broad back.

Sherlock broke from cover the moment Moran was away, and made immediately for the harness horse's mate, which was fresher than their own milling, anxious mounts. Despite John's cries for him to "Wait!" he was off in pursuit.

John spared a moment to see that Jun, while winded and bleeding, was not in danger. 'See to your father!' he shouted, catching up the reins of his own horse. His body, earlier aching with the weariness of horseback travel, did not feel anything except the sing and roar of adrenalin. He urged the poor beast to gallop in the wake of Sherlock Holmes and their deadly enemy.

He may not have caught up to them, fresh as their horses were, but a horse trained to harness is not a horse trained to the saddle. Stiff-necked, flat of withers and heavy of shoulder, they were bred to drag, not to carry – neither beast fathomed anything but the broadest signal from their riders to turn, to gather speed or to slow. Their alarm made them even less responsive.

Sherlock and Moran's horses galloped ahead of John's, cutting south, away from the lake and across the railroad tracks, then flying with unwise speed over treacherous ground towards the river they had followed with Li Jun on their way there.

No gunplay occurred. Without saddles or stirrups, each man was concentrating on clinging on with their legs to their beast's heaving sides, holding on to the reins and trying to maintain some control. John, even on his tired animal, began to gain ground.

Then Moran's horse stumbled and jerked to a stop, shooting his rider off his broad, sweaty back and onto the hard ground. Moran scrabbled to his knees, raised his pistol and pulled the trigger, only to hear an empty click.

Sherlock slowed his own mount and with much more grace, swung his leg across the horse's withers and slid to the earth.

'It's over, Colonel Moran,' Sherlock said, standing tall and hardly even short of breath.

'So you think, Holmes, but the night's yet young and I've fire in my belly enough to kill you with my bare hands.'

'You're welcome to try,' said Sherlock, within a toucher of baring his teeth, 'None yet have managed the deed.'

Moran lurched to his feet and glowered at Sherlock. 'You're a mite impressed with yourself.'

John reined his horse to a halt and left the beast heaving for breath as he dismounted and drew his revolver once more.

Moran grinned at him like a savage animal. 'And here's the inevitable Doctor Watson. Adair adds another betrayal to his list, in not killing you.'

'Not for the lack of trying,' John admitted darkly.

'He never was made for the hands-on work,' said Moran disparagingly. He glanced towards the river and his eyes narrowed.

In the falling light, John and Sherlock both saw the dark shape slithering in the grass. The temperature was cooling as the sun began to set: the snakes were stirring.

'Step out of there,' said Sherlock, John backing up the words with his gun, 'I'd hate for a serpent to finish you before the hangman can.'

'I'm not afraid of snakes,' said Moran, 'I used to catch 'em with my bare hands in India, pit vipers, cobras and all.'

'Like calling to like, no doubt,' said Sherlock.

'No doubt,' said Moran, as the shape slithered by, avoiding him by passing between him and Sherlock.

In one swift movement, Moran scooped it up in two hands and flung the suddenly enraged and coiling reptile across the mere yards which separated them. John fired, but Moran was already running for the harness beast Sherlock had ridden – hard to ride but still fresher and better than the winded animals that shied from him. Moran mounted, kicked and shouted, and the horse galloped wildly off into the darkness, Moran clinging to its back.

John began to give chase, but halted at Sherlock's sudden cry of alarm. He saw the black-scaled serpent attached to Sherlock's forearm through the cuff of his jacket. Saw Sherlock seize the vile thing near the head, pluck it free and fling it from him, where it coiled and reared, revealing a scarlet belly, ready to strike again.

John had never considered himself a crack shot, but with strange, icy calm, he shot this target clean through its wicked head before it could attack.

Then he ran to Sherlock's side as Sherlock, in the midst of dragging off his jacket and shirt to inspect the damage, wobbled on his legs and folded to the earth.

Chapter Thirteen

John whipped Sherlock's coat away, then pushed Sherlock to the ground with firm hands on his chest and supporting his back.

'Lie still,' he commanded, 'Let me see.'

'It's nothing,' began Sherlock, but he was deathly pale already, and did as his doctor bid him.

John pulled Sherlock's sleeve up to find the puncture wounds in his forearm – one deeper than the other, the snake's fangs disrupted by the cuff of the coat and shirt.

'It took me at an angle,' Sherlock explained, surprised to hear his own breath shaking, 'I raised my arm to fend it off.'

'You must stay calm,' John said quietly, with reassuring confidence. He'd retrieved his pocket knife and cut the shirt to tear it further so he could twist the cloth into a tourniquet around Sherlock's upper arm. His grasping hand found a short, slender stick, which he twisted into the cloth to tighten it.

'The Tibetans meditate,' said Sherlock, watching John work, 'It slows the heartrate. I imagine that would be very useful, to reduce the spread of the poison.'

'It would, if you know the trick of it.'

Sherlock smiled wanly. 'I do.'

'Then by all means meditate. I must get the water.' He laid Sherlock's hand across his chest and ran to his horse – the canteen was on the saddle, thank God, and his medical kit at the top of the saddlebag. He snatched them both up, shaking the canteen. Half full. Enough to begin with.

John flung open the roll of instruments and took up a scalpel. 'This will hurt, but it can't be helped.' John held the small knife steady in one hand, while with the other hand he braced Sherlock's wounded forearm. 'Ready?'

Sherlock nodded, his eyes never leaving John's steady hands.

John swiftly made two small incisions on either side of the fang marks – a cut across the bite would force poison further into the body. Blood welled and spilled and then John's mouth closed over the new wounds and he sucked. He spat a mouthful of blood into the grass, then sealed the wounds under his lips and sucked again. Spat. Sucked. Spat. Spat a second time and a third to clear his mouth from blood and venom – it wouldn't do to make himself sick now, by accidentally swallowing the poison. He snatched up the canteen and took a small mouthful. He poured water carefully over the wounds, irrigating them further while he swilled his mouthful and spat it out. He took another mouthful, swilled as he continued to irrigate the poison from the injury, then spat. He poured water into the hollow of his hand and scrubbed at his bloodstained moustache as well, rinsing it clear. It was the first time he'd ever regretted the thing.

'Sherlock,' he said in a clear, calm voice, 'Look at me.'

Sherlock raised his eyes. In them John saw perfect faith. John brushed his hand across Sherlock's cheek.

'I'll carry you to the river. I need to clean the wound further, but we must keep your circulation as placid as we can. Keep on with your meditation.'

With that he lifted Sherlock into his arms and carried him the fifteen steps to the river. The sandy incline of the bank was not too hard to navigate with his precious burden, and he lay Sherlock in the water, ensuring the bleeding arm was in the flow so that poisoned blood continued to be rinsed away.

John took another, larger mouthful of water and rinsed his own mouth and moustache more thoroughly as he filled the canteen from the river and then held it to Sherlock's lips.

'You must drink and urinate as much as possible to flush the venom out,' he said in that firm tone. He held Sherlock's head while he drank, then let him rest on the bank again.

'How do you feel?' he asked, taking Sherlock's pulse, feeling his forehead for his temperature.

'Weak,' admitted Sherlock, placidly, 'My limbs are all trembling. It's a curious phenomenon. I'll make notes, later.'

'Yes, you shall.' John brushed Sherlock's dark fringe, damp from feverish sweat, away from his eyes. He moved to Sherlock's injured side and knelt in the water as he released the pressure of the tourniquet on his upper arm for a few moments, then tightened it once more.

He helped Sherlock to further drink, then took off and bundled up his own half-soaked coat to act as a pillow under Sherlock's head. 'Keep drinking,' he instructed, 'I must fetch things from my kit.'

John ran up the bank to his instruments, which he gathered all at once and carried back to Sherlock's side, where he helped Sherlock drink some more and then refilled the canteen.

Blood flowed from Sherlock's arm in stark red ribbons from the two cuts, swirling away to nothing in the water.

'Can you urinate?' John asked as he searched in his kit. There. The last of the laudanum.

Sherlock was silent, and John held Sherlock's chin in his hands. 'Sherlock, can you hear me?'

'My hearing is perfectly adequate, thank you, Doctor.'

John's lips quirked in an odd smile. 'You're already hip deep in the river, Sherlock. The suit's already ruined and your tailor can't possibly berate you for it now.'

'It appears to be a thing more easily said than done, however,' said Sherlock, annoyed at his own discomfiture.

'It can be so,' agreed John gently, 'Don't distress yourself over it. Let me…' He held the laudanum to Sherlock's lips so that he could drink the small dose, and followed it with more water. 'That will help to slow your heart and relax you. And now…' Having made Sherlock comfortable, he reached into the water to unfasten the buttons of Sherlock's trousers and then untie his drawers.

'This is not how I imagined it would be, when next you had your hands on me,' said Sherlock drily, looking steadfastly at John's ear.

'Nor I, but the time after this will doubtless be more appealing.' Having freed Sherlock from the confines of his clothes, he released his patient's private parts – any arousal at this point was unlikely but would certainly be unhelpful, and he was kneeling by Sherlock's head again, helping him to drink. For a moment Sherlock's body was tense, then he relaxed as finally his body passed water, carrying away some of the toxins with it.

For a time, that was how they lay, with the sinking sun splashing colours across the few clouds that scudded across the sky. John cradled Sherlock's head on his lap and gave him sips of water while he smoothed his fingers across Sherlock's forehead and through his dark hair. Periodically, he released the tourniquet to maintain circulation, checked Sherlock's vital signs and loosened the constriction altogether. He tore the shredded fabric free and wiped the cuts and puncture wounds in Sherlock's arm with it.

'We managed to lose my carbolic soap when we bathed last time. I don't even have cologne or alcohol to use as an antiseptic for these injuries,' he said quietly, 'I lost much of my medical kit on the *Lenore Ann* when young Delancey made an attempt on my life. Oh my dear fellow, don't be concerned, for here I am, aren't I? There, you roll your eyes at me. That's more like it. When I'm satisfied we have eliminated as much venom as we can, I'll build a fire and boil water to clean the cuts. I can use eucalyptus leaves to make an antiseptic poultice that will do for now. The natives near Ballarat used it and other plants for all kinds of medicines, and the Indians and Afghanis too. I was always fascinated by such remedies, even if they seemed unscientific.'

'The properties of plants are the key of all medicines,' said Sherlock, calm and not slurring at all.

'So they are,' agreed John, 'And so I'll do what I can until I may better treat the wound. It's as well this river is clean. The water is very clear and very fresh tasting, isn't it? Here, drink. I'd be happier if you passed more of it before I attempt a fire.'

Darkness fell before John was satisfied. Sherlock began to protest that he was well, but his limbs remained weak from the shock – a fact revealed when Sherlock attempted to stand. He managed it, but barely.

169

'You have always had the constitution of an ox,' John admonished him, a hand under his elbow, 'But I knew from the moment I saw you that you have tried your body to the limits. For once in your life, will you allow me to be the expert?'

Sherlock shuddered all over and John had to wrap an arm across his back, and sling Sherlock's arm across his shoulders, to keep him upright.

'Perhaps this once,' conceded Sherlock.

'Ass,' said John affectionately. He helped Sherlock to the dry bank and then to recline once more. He stripped Sherlock of his wet clothes, bar his vest and drawers, then set about building a fire, using the matches. He rummaged in his kit and found a tin mug in which to boil water, and pulled out his last clean clothes.

Finally, he stripped Sherlock of the wet underwear and helped him into John's dry replacements, He tore up his last clean shirt, cutting some of the cloth into small squares which he boiled. Once they'd cooled enough, he used them with tweezers to wipe over Sherlock's wounds. The bleeding had ceased some time ago and the cuts appeared clean.

John emptied the mug, boiled fresh water and this time placed young eucalyptus leaves in it. When sufficiently stewed, he made a poultice of them which he bandaged to Sherlock's arm with strips of his torn shirt. 'There. We must wait until the morning to return to Ararat, but you'll be all right until then.'

Finally, he saw to the horses, who had already calmed enough to graze and drink, standing close to each other. John unsaddled his horse – he took the blanket to Sherlock to keep him warm – and returned to rub the animal down with fistfuls of long grass. He did the same for the other, washed his hands, his face and the mug in the river, stripped at last out of his own wet boots and trousers, and sat down wearily by Sherlock's side in unbuttoned waistcoat, shirt and drawers, damp from the waist down. The night remained warm, but he built the fire up in any case. He used cooled ashes at the fringe of the little fire to clean his teeth, rubbing granular soot vigorously against teeth and gums with his forefinger, then rinsing his mouth again. Then, with the last of their provisions, he made strong, sweet bush tea in the mug. He steadied Sherlock with a hand to his back while Sherlock sipped on the brew.

'I'm sorry there's nothing to make a broth for you. '

'I have come this far and survived, thanks to your excellent care,' said Sherlock gently, 'I will survive another day.'

'That would be ideal. God could not be cruel enough to deliver you back to me and then take you away again within the week.'

John fell broodingly silent then, his hands folded in his lap. With a grimace, he pulled at the chain on his waistcoat and brought out his watch. Water trickled from the casing, from where it had become submerged in the river while he was seeing to Sherlock's care. He opened the watch to let the rest of the water drain out. Even in the dim light, Sherlock could see how John's moustache bristled as he pursed his lips.

'This is not God punishing us,' Sherlock said sternly, but a whisper of anxiety was in it as well. 'That watch is not fate. *It is only a watch.* Tell me you do not believe such a thing.'

'No, my dear, I don't believe that God is punishing us.' John agreed with a small smile, stroking Sherlock's cheek with a fingertip, 'This is Fate telling me to cherish you. And I shall. For all the rest of our days, which will be many.' His smile widened, to Sherlock's puzzlement, and he added, 'In any case, the serpent in Eden was the devil's work, as this one was Moran's.'

'Between Grimsby Roylott's pet and this new encounter,' said Sherlock, closing his eyes again, 'I do not think I'm fond of snakes.'

'Then I shall stay awake and make sure no more come calling. I recall these red-bellied things liked the rivers. But not fires. They avoid human contact if they can. We shall be safe enough.'

'Really, John,' murmured Sherlock, more sleepily now, 'You're quite the outdoorsman.'

'Between the goldfields and the wars, I've had my fill of wide open spaces,' John told him fondly, 'Give me London, a hansom cab and a good puzzle any time.'

'There's my John Watson.'

Sherlock's eyes flew open as he felt lips on his, and the soft bristles of John's moustache against his upper lip, then closed them to better concentrate on the sensation.

'There's my Sherlock Holmes,' whispered John.

Thus they settled in the thankfully warm night. John stared into the fire and stared and stared. Now that the crisis was past, old battlefield responses were flaring up. Clenched jaw, trembling hands, the bleak knowledge of what the day had almost cost him.

He is well, he is well, he is well. Much of the venom did not enter his body. Most of that which did enter was quickly extracted. He's weak because of fatigue and only a little because of the poison. He will live. He lives. I haven't lost him again. I have not.

He curled his fingers into fists to stay the impulse to reach out for Sherlock and take his pulse again. He'd never been one to fuss or give in to fancies. He would not begin now.

But then he felt long, cool fingers settling over his fist; squeezing the tense knuckles that flexed and drove his fingernails to make crescented dents in his palm. Sherlock rubbed his thumb over John's hand soothingly.

'All is well,' Sherlock said quietly into the dark night, 'We are well.'

'I know,' said John, relaxing his hand to entwine with Sherlock's, 'It's a reaction. The after-effects of adrenalin. Though I swear, if I once get my hands on Sebastian Moran, he's in for a thrashing.' He held Sherlock's hand in his lap. 'Rest and restore your strength, my dear. I'll keep watch.' *For snakes and villains and encroaching cold. I will keep them all at bay.*

'You are the best of men,' said Sherlock, tone playful, making John laugh.

'I'm a grumpy old soldier.'

'And you have plighted your troth to a reckless adventurer who has on occasion rather less sense than a yearling colt.'

'Well, then, we are perfectly matched,' declared John.

'We are indeed.'

'Now sleep, unless you want to prove your point.'

Sherlock, amusement softening his features, relaxed and obeyed.

John remained vigilant, feeding the fire and watching for danger, periodically checking that Sherlock's sleep was undisturbed by further symptoms of illness. From time to time he rested a hand on Sherlock's, to feel the warmth of his skin – and he gave thanks under this open sky, under these kindly stars, for their deliverance.

Sherlock woke hours later as John shook him gently by the shoulder. 'We have company,' murmured John. False dawn was beginning to illuminate the sky.

Ranged about them were eight men from a native hunting party – perhaps the one they had seen earlier. They were dressed in curious combinations of native skins and threadbare trousers and shirts, though their bodies were marked in traditional paint and scars. They carried spears and bulging woven grass bags. A wallaby tail protruded from one of the bags. The hunters stared down at the two men with frank curiosity.

'You fellahs lost, eh?' asked one of the men.

'My friend was bitten by a snake,' John said. He'd pulled on his dried trousers and still-damp boots.

The man waved at the other clothes hung about on bushes to dry. 'An' you put him in the river to wash the poison out? You a smart *gubbah*.' He said something to another of his party. The latter lifted up the body of the snake on the end of his spear. 'You a good shot.'

'I'm a *lucky* shot,' said John.

The man laughed, told the others what John had said. They all laughed too. Sherlock watched closely and said nothing.

'Can you help us?' asked John.

'We gotta get home soon.'

'If you'll help me to get my friend on a horse, that's all we need. Please.'

'You got good manners for a whitefellah,' said the hunter through narrow eyes.

John didn't reply, but met the man's gaze with as open and honest an expression as was at his disposal. The hunter spoke to his companions and the next moment, both horses were led up to them.

'Best you don't sleep any more by the river, *gubbah*,' said the hunter, 'The redbellies come here to drink in the day.' The little gathering laughed again, good-naturedly ribbing their obvious idiocy.

With much fussing and amusement at the strangeness of the white men, John saddled his horse while Sherlock managed to dress himself, despite residual weakness. The hunting party helped Sherlock into the saddle first, then gave John a leg up behind him. They looped the carriage horse's reins around the pommel.

'Whitefellah town that way.' The hunter pointed north west. 'Where them trains come along. You find your fellahs soon.'

'Thank you.' John's voice was infused with the warmth of his gratitude. 'Should I pay you? For passage on your lands?'

The hunter stared at him quizzically, then waved expansively ahead of them with wry generosity. 'Nah, *gubbah*. You go on. You free to go on Djabwurrung land.' He grinned at John. 'You not a bad fellah.'

John couldn't help but feel a little patronised, like a child let off a chore for not knowing better. Then he noticed one of the other hunters whispering to a friend, both observing the gleaming chain of his watch, which he'd automatically replaced in its pocket.

'The watch is broken,' he said to the hunter, 'It was soaked in the river.'

'Washed it with him friend, eh?'

'I'm afraid so.'

The hunter smirked, told the others, and there was another round of merriment at the expense of the *gubbahs*.

'My brother say that shiny is pretty for his wife.'

John handed the watch to the hunter. 'Here, then. It has been an anchor and a weight around my heart, keeping me from better harbours. Take it. Keep it, sell it, dismantle it for decoration. Do whatever you will with it. I hope it brings you better fortune than it ever gave the Watsons.'

The hunter dangled the fob watch on its chain, watching it catch the soft morning light as true dawn caught up with them. Then he tossed it across to his brother, who caught it and stowed it in a basket with the wallaby tail.

'Thank you again,' said John.

'And be aware,' Sherlock added, speaking at last, 'A very dangerous white man escaped from us last night, on a horse like that,' he nodded at the carriage horse. 'His name is Sebastian Moran and he is a killer. He won't hesitate to harm you, if he thinks it will do him good.'

The hunter shrugged. 'Whitefellah business,' he said, as though that encompassed everything. With a few words, he and his hunting party were off again, walking easily across the light-flushed landscape.

John encouraged their mount north, alongside the river and towards Ararat, the carriage horse ambling at their side. John kept one arm about Sherlock's waist, despite the fact that Sherlock was perfectly secure in the saddle and much better rested than John himself. Still, Sherlock made no protest. Perhaps he was as satisfied with their proximity as John was, his back flush to John's front.

Half way to the railroad tracks, they were met by a small party on horseback led by a police constable, sent by Beth the Cook to find them.

Chapter Fourteen

The doctor was at the Crosby house when John and Sherlock arrived. He saw to swabbing Sherlock's wounds with antiseptic and wrapping them in clean bandages. John took the opportunity to clean his teeth and mouth with a patent powder, and to properly wash his face and moustache with soap.

Sherlock watched John from his position at the kitchen table while John saw to his ablutions at a basin of warm water. He knew before John set out his shaving kit that the shave would never happen. Fatigue had set his hands to trembling, as they had last night when the crisis was past. He hadn't seen John react like that since their earliest days, when his new fellow lodger was still recovering from injury and illness. Sherlock ignored the local doctor's questions as he assessed John Watson's response – stress, a post-adrenalin reaction, physical exhaustion. Sherlock cursed that he'd fallen asleep during the night. He hadn't meant to. His years away from London had played havoc with his discipline.

Then he saw John's reflection in the little shaving mirror on its stand, smiling reassuringly at him. Sherlock found he didn't mind his loss of discipline so much after all. The breach had left room for John to step into it.

Grooming his refreshed moustache into line, John returned to the kitchen table, where the irritating country doctor pronounced Sherlock was fit, thanks to the swift aid he'd received. Sherlock could have told him that fifteen minutes ago.

The cook brought them bowls of hot Scottish porridge, salted and rich with butter, along with thick pieces of buttered bread and a pot of strong tea. Sherlock found he was ravenous, but he ate slowly. He was entertained by John packing away his meal with swift but tidy efficiency.

While they ate, the constable advised them of what had transpired since they had gone in pursuit of Moran.

Poor James Crosby was dead, having throttled himself out of terror of the red leech.

'Revolting as it was, the leech was unlikely to have actually entered Crosby's ear as threatened,' said Sherlock thoughtfully, 'I certainly never found a sign of such torment on Moran's other victims. The leech was an instrument of terror for Moran to extract information. Horrible enough, but not more than that, I think.'

'We shan't know now,' said Constable Pace, 'The girl – the Chinese lad turned out to be a girl – beat the thing to a pulp with a rock.'

'Ah. Li Jun. How is she?' Sherlock asked.

'Upstairs, sleeping,' said Pace, 'I thought of arresting her when I thought she was a him, but Mr Li begged her pardon, and since he saved my mam once, with his Chinese medicine, I owed him a favour. Beth says Miss Li ain't broken a law here, and maybe that's right.' He frowned, as though suspicious that any woman so dressed could truly be innocent of any wrongdoing. 'And Mrs Mary Li, in any case, cried so hard when I said I might arrest her girl that the doctor made me say I wouldn't.'

'You acted wisely, constable,' said Sherlock, 'Li Jun has committed no wrongs in this country.'

Pace peered at him. 'What was your name again?' he demanded.

'Sigerson,' said Sherlock easily, 'And this is my friend, Dr Sacker.'

'That's not what Beth told me. She told me you were the famous Mr Sherlock Holmes.'

'Famous, is he?' Sherlock arched an eyebrow, 'And so he'd claim some credit for your work last night, rescuing Mr Wen Li and his long lost daughter from the black villain who murdered James Crosby?'

Pace pursed his lips thoughtfully.

'Well, Mr Sigerson,' he said at last, 'I do get your meaning. If there had been a Mr Holmes here, no doubt he'd have had more to say.'

'Such as the importance of a telegram sent without delay to the authorities in Melbourne to keep watch for one Colonel Sebastian Moran, who is certainly attempting to flee the country.'

'Moran,' Pace wrote down the name, 'Wanted for the murders of Mr Crosby, Mr Culver and young Tommy Bailey, as well as the deadly assault on Mr Garcia, which'll be another murder charge soon enough, Doc Ainslie says. Right. Now you'd best tell me the thing from your end, gentlemen.'

John gave a report as succinctly as any army report, ending with, 'Then Moran hefted the red bellied snake with his bare hands and set it on Mr Sigerson. We were forced to camp the night while he recovered from the subsequent bite. A group of native hunters gave us assistance this morning.'

Sherlock gave him a sidelong look, but said nothing until later, when Pace had left with their statements.

'Your modesty is not a virtue, John.'

John shrugged. 'Nor is it relevant. He had no need of the details, and I'm in sore need of sleep.'

They were despatched to the only spare room – poor Crosby was laid out on his own bed, awaiting the undertaker, while Wen sat by his wife's bedside and their daughter took up the first guest room. In the absence of a mistress of the house who could decide things, Beth had arranged things as efficiently as possible.

'Do you mind awfully sharing the second guest room?' she'd asked anxiously, 'Tis a big enough bed that you won't disturb one another, and Doctor Ainslie says you both need rest.'

John appeared too tired to form much in the way of sentences now that the policeman had gone. Sherlock replied soberly, 'My friend and I are old campaigners and we shall manage.'

'Of course, sir,' said Beth kindly, noting John's exhaustion, 'And... thank you for trying to catch that villain who... who...k-killed...' The staunch woman faltered at last, but mastered her grief once more. 'The law shall catch up to that devil, and no mistake,' she said vehemently, 'In the meantime, you have saved Mr Li and brought his and Mrs Mary's daughter home. That is enough to thank you for. I'll wake you later for supper, but ring if you need anything. If you need the doctor again...'

'Doctor Watson is my physician,' said Sherlock firmly, 'And once he is rested I'll need no other. Thank you.'

Alone in the guest room, Sherlock disrobed down to his drawers and donned one of the late Mr Crosby's nightshirts provided for them. He assisted John, so sluggish in his movements, to the same.

'Here you are, my dear fellow.'

'Are you not sleeping too?' John asked as Sherlock helped him under the covers, 'You need your rest. You're still recovering.'

'In good time,' Sherlock told him. He pulled a chair up beside the bed with his good arm. He sat in it, by John's pillow, and stroked John's hair.

'You must rest, my dear chap,' John insisted.

Sherlock's expression threatened argument, but then he crossed to the other side of the bed and climbed in beside John, sitting up. 'Will this satisfy you?' he asked, cocking an eyebrow.

Even through his exhaustion, John's eye glittered with impudent humour. 'Until we can safely satisfy ourselves in other ways, it will do.'

Sherlock rested his hand upon John's shoulder, his austere features warm with amused tenderness. 'We may have to be very patient.' He sobered. 'We have, after all, waited thirteen years, and I learned to school my appetites, such as they were, long before then.'

A crease appeared between John's brows as the statement caught on the edges of his thoughts. Sherlock watched the shadow of confusion become consideration, and a touch of disappointment smoothed away under fond acceptance.

You misunderstand my comment regarding my appetites, and yet you accept me. As you have always accepted me as an unconventional man.

'John, you are drawing erroneous conclusions again.'

'You never were one for... expressions of physical love...' began John, in the most understanding of tones, resigned but also tender. 'I'm by your side, which is more than I dared hope. I make no demands but that.'

'I said "such as they *were*". My appetites may not have been as robust as yours always seemed to be. However...' He rubbed his thumb firmly against John's scarred shoulder. '...increase of appetite has grown by what it feeds on. I have been a more than willing participant in our recent amorous activities. I look forward to more of them. But there's no profit in speaking of those at present. You need rest and I need to think.'

John's whole expression became suffused with almost radiant affection, which Sherlock found deeply affecting to see. So many years of John smothering such expressions, and here they were, unshielded at last. It prompted an unshielded expression of his own, feelings too, that he'd worked for years to master, to put aside, for the work and to avoid distraction. To avoid a repeat of the confused despair he'd experienced when Victor rejected him.

Yet John was not Victor, and not a distraction. John was part of the great adventure.

Sherlock bent to kiss John's forehead. 'Sleep,' he commanded.

*

John stirred many hours later, to the delicious scent of hot soup and fresh bread.

'I have chased the maid out,' Sherlock told him from the bedside chair, 'She was in danger of fussing.' Sherlock, clean-shaven, was fully clothed once more, in his own suit that was the worse for its harsh use in recent days, but well brushed and the few rips well mended. John's suit, in similar repair, was laid over the wing chair in the corner. The household had busied themselves to distract them from grief.

John scrubbed his hands over his face and through his hair, trying to rearrange the frightful mess. 'Have you been here all this while?'

'Most of it,' Sherlock rose to transfer the tray from the side table to John's lap. 'I have spoken again with Constable Pace and made arrangements for our return to Melbourne on tomorrow's train. Our belongings have been retrieved from the horses.' He waved a hand towards the wardrobe, indicating that it contained their meagre belongings, 'And I have further arranged with a local trader for the horse Miss Li stole to be returned to its owners with some little sum for compensation, in return for our own pair.'

'Any news of Moran?' asked John as he ate.

'None. I won't be surprised if he evades capture. He's a wily fellow and policing of the ports is even more lackadaisical in the colonies than in London. I have despatched a telegram to Mycroft to advise him of the situation. Adair will have to be watched. Moran will doubtless be bent on revenging himself there, until he can make another play for our lives.'

'Won't he be awaiting us in Melbourne?'

'It's a possibility, but not only are we forewarned now, he's wanted for four murders – Garcia died a few hours ago. No. Australia is not the frontier territory it was and he's made himself too hot for even this vast land to hold him. A smarter man would flee to Africa or the East, but while Moran is cunning, he's also subject to irrational motivations like revenge. Why else pursue Miss Li all this way?'

'The diamond,' pointed out John reasonably. He pushed the tray aside and got out of bed. His underthings were not in the best state, but in the absence of anything clean they'd have to do for now. He was more pleased to find his shaving kit had been brought to the room along with a fresh jug of warm water. He set about shaving as Sherlock spoke. Sherlock noted with satisfaction that the tremor had abandoned John's hands at last.

'There were greater treasures in Moriarty's holdings, although Adair may well have seized upon those already. Moran learned of this betrayal and pursued it with more single-mindedness than even our old friend Toby could summon. This is personal to him, as are we. If he can't despatch us or Miss Li, then he will direct his tenacity towards the other target of his rage. I've no doubt he'll turn his attention back to us when he feels he has more chance of success.'

'There's a cheering thought,' said John grimly, 'But he'll find us ready for him.'

John dressed and insisted on checking the state of Sherlock's health, though he was satisfied with a quick inspection and Sherlock's statement that he suffered no worrying symptoms of infection.

In the parlour, where they joined the shocked and diminished household, Sherlock found an argument in progress.

'The White Dragon is ours, the diamond is not,' insisted Li Wen, 'It has brought enough ill luck to this family.'

Li Jun appeared as neither man had ever seen her – her delicate frame draped in a fine dress, her striking face clean and her dark hair twisted into a feminine style. Her eyes blazed in a ferocity they both knew – an expression, Sherlock noted, that was not new to either of her parents. It seemed Miss Li had always had a fiery spirit. Well, of course. She had relentlessly pursued her goal for many years and won her way home, although the cost had been terrible.

'I suffered for that diamond, Baba! We have all suffered for it. It belongs to us, now.' She turned her bright, wild glare to Sherlock. 'You placed this in my hands. You gave it back to me. It's *mine*.' Her right hand was clutched around the little parcel of silk which contained the Hortensia Diamond.

'I was retained once by the French Government to retrieve that diamond.' Sherlock held out his hand and, although she was angry, Jun placed the diamond into his palm.

Sherlock unwrapped the jewel and held it up between thumb and forefinger. Sparkling light danced off the pink stone.

He tossed it to John, who snatched it from the air and inspected it.

'You recall the case, Watson?'

'It was the cause of great frustration.'

'Indeed. Our intelligence was that the stone had been cut and sold as six separate stones. Even were those stones to be recovered, the Hortensia Diamond as a piece is no more.'

'I recall.'

'This therefore cannot be the Hortensia Diamond.'

Sherlock watched as John shot him a look and then, as always, complied.

'I can't see how it could be. This stone has similarities, but the flaw is insurmountable. It is one stone, and not six.'

'Exactly so.'

John offered it back to Sherlock, who threw it carelessly back to Jun.

She closed her fist around it, her eyes alight with triumph. Yet her father protested and, seated by the fire, her mother was distressed.

'It doesn't belong to us,' said Li Wen.

'I can't see to whom else it belongs,' said Sherlock, 'Nor do I intend to squander time or energy on finding out. Your family has suffered much at the hands of these blackguards. You may take the jewel in recompense, or not. I wash my hands of it.'

'Oh, my dear,' said Mary Li, with a catch in her voice, 'Let us think on it, at least. We must see to James's household, and poor Mr Garcia's mother, as well as Tommy Bailey's family. Surely we can use it for some good for those who've been hurt?'

Sherlock was not interested in the further discussion. John followed him into the front garden, where they strolled in the dry air and marvelled that anyone had ever convinced roses to grow in it.

'The sooner we're back in London, the better,' Sherlock said, 'We must bring an end to this business.'

*

The train journey to Melbourne was free of incident and by early afternoon they had visited shipping offices to book passage on a steamship to London two days hence under their *noms de guerre*. Next they stopped at the grand post office on Elizabeth Street to telegram Mycroft the news of their impending departure.

Mrs Gallagher of the Collins Street lodgings greeted them in her flapping way, preoccupied with the finishing touches to her art and not the least bit concerned that the gentleman, Mr Sigerson, intended to share Doctor Sacker's room for a few days.

'I don't have a free room – Mr Carr is here from Bendigo for the exhibition and has the second room for a week. The third will be occupied before the showing if Mr Lafarge is true to his word, and he's usually quite reliable. Your room has a large bed, Dr Sacker, if you have no objection to sharing it. Some of our set share beds all the time, and it's not like they have to.' She waved a paintbrush overhead then pushed some strands of hair behind her ear with the stained end of it. 'Why anyone should object is beyond me – grown men do worse things from sheer stupidity and greed and there's little enough love in the world. But there, I've shocked you. You think that the colonies have never heard of Bohemia.'

John was too amazed to reply, and Sherlock too circumspect. They retired to John's room, where John unearthed fresh clothing from his untouched trunk and retrieved funds secreted against later need from the locked despatch box. His hat had been abandoned as beyond salvation, but he had packed another. They were both clad now in fresh drawers and clean suits. Sherlock contrived to let down hems on the trousers and coat John lent him, so that he wouldn't look like a vaudeville clown with his bony ankles and wrists exposed.

Satisfied that he made a passable gentlemen, Sherlock glanced across to John, sitting on a chair and holding a letter he'd retrieved from the pages of a notebook. He examined John's posture and expression for a time, before seeking to understand the paper at which John stared with such preoccupation. John's thumb and finger rubbed absently at his waistcoat where the watch chain had once hung. He tugged lightly at the fabric, as though the absent weight of it was a curious irritant.

'We shall go and pay our respects, if you like,' said Sherlock.

'It's in St Kilda.' John frowned and looked up at him. 'You know what this letter contains?'

'It's the letter you received when your brother's watch was sent to you.'

'Surely you haven't read it. I kept it locked up with my papers.'

'I haven't seen it before today. I have not read it. But I have read *you*.'

John smiled, though the expression was a little weary. 'As you do.' He lifted the single sheet of thin paper, the old wrinkles in it pressed almost smooth from its five years spent within heavier pages. 'Henry's friend, who sent me the watch and saw to his burial, wrote to me. He didn't say so, but it's clear that Marcus Appleby was not merely Henry's *friend*.'

'No.'

'I daren't show you this at the time. Henry's whole story would have come out and I was not prepared for you to know it then. But I was glad, even so, that my brother was not entirely alone at the last. Poor Henry.' John replaced the paper neatly inside the notebook. 'I'd like to pay my respects to him. I'd be glad of your company, if you'd like to come.'

They encountered Mrs Gallagher in the hall as they departed.

'I'm hosting a supper in the parlour tonight. You're most welcome to attend, Doctor Sacker, Mr Sigerson,' said Mrs Gallagher, 'George'll be on the piano and his Robbie sings a treat. Pippin will be sure to do some of his tricks – my friend Mr Norris plays at Ned Kelly and shoots Pippin the Police Dog with his finger, and Pippin, bless his snaggletoothed head, falls down dead like a trooper and can only be revived with a bit of sausage. He's terribly smart for a mutt – Pippin, I mean. Oh, you're off. Good. I have a painting to finish!'

John laughed at Sherlock's mildly shell-shocked expression as they took their promenade into the city proper. 'She is rather a force of nature,' John conceded, 'But your brother gave me a letter of introduction, so I must assume that she's discreet enough.'

A cable tram took them all the way from Melbourne's bustling centre to the seaside town of St Kilda. They alighted at the junction and walked east until they found the cemetery gates. A gardener was at work on this warm afternoon and was able to advise where to find the grave of an Englishman buried there in 1888.

As the sun westered in Australia's hot mid-October sky, John found his brother's grave, obscured beneath a eucalypt and marred with webs, weeds and bird droppings. He stood side-by-side with Sherlock to regard the inscription.

In Memory of
My friend
Henry Gordon Watson
15 April 1847 – 3 May 1888

It was necessary to crouch and clear away the weeds to read the epitaph.

> "'Tis better to have loved and lost
> Than never to have loved at all."

'Henry was fond of Tennyson,' said John quietly. 'We learned *The Charge of the Light Brigade* by heart. He loved to perform *The Kraken* with his arms waving about, trying to make it seem there were more of them, to make me laugh.' He reached out to touch his fingers to the neglected stone. Marcus had long gone and no-one remained to tend the grave.

John knelt and pulled more weeds away from it while Sherlock watched him.

Henry's tragic example had made John so reluctant to act on his desires; it had led the doctor to follow the path of least resistance and marry Mary Morstan. He supposed Henry Watson was not truly to blame, but Sherlock couldn't feel warmly towards the man.

Kneeling, John said, 'Are we alone, Sherlock? I can detect no-one, but your senses are more acute than mine.'

Sherlock listened. 'It's too warm at his hour for most to be about. The gardener takes a rest by the gates. No other mourners are here. For a while at least, yes. We are quite alone.'

John brushed detritus from his hands, rose and stood close to Sherlock.

'His fate led to mine,' John said softly, 'I was sent away, but it's true that I ran from myself, too. I never thought myself to want courage, but for many years, I did. I almost ruined our chance with that want.'

'Don't be harsh on yourself. I did very little to encourage you to take such a risk. You thought me unwilling or uninterested.'

John's hand looped through the crook of Sherlock's elbow, as friends could yet do.

Sherlock regarded his dear friend's solemn countenance. 'I must apologise again, for how I upset you when I announced my conclusions from your brother's watch,' he said, 'And I'm sorry, too, that you had to give up the piece for my sake.'

John eyes were not filled with sorrow, but affection. 'That watch was weighted with so much evil memory that it was a burden and a barrier that kept me from you for thirteen years. Now it and the barrier it represented have gone and I'll never allow anything to keep me from you again.' He glanced about then, alert and curious. 'You're certain no-one is about?'

'Not a living soul.'

They quirked smiles at each other at the macabre reference to the graveyard, then John took Sherlock's hand in his in a more intimate gesture. 'I'm about to commit an act of outrageous sentiment,' he said, 'And you will allow it.'

Sherlock's eyes sparkled teasingly, but he only nodded. John faced the grave.

'Henry,' said John to the headstone, 'This is my very dear friend, Sherlock Holmes, of whom I once wrote you, and whom I love most ardently.'

He cleared his throat, feeling foolish, although Sherlock had let the little speech occur without comment.

'It's nothing but the truth,' said John, 'And I'm glad to tell *someone* besides yourself of the depth of my feelings for you, even if he is dead. He'd have understood.'

John released Sherlock's hand to unnecessarily straighten his collar and smooth down his moustache with his thumb.

'There,' he said decisively, 'I have made my declaration before the only witness who mattered to me. I am yours. We'll go home and finish this thing with Moran. We'll return to Baker Street and we'll manage everything else, one way or another.'

'You are determined on that point?'

'If, as I have said, you'll have me.'

'Oh yes. You may count on that.'

An impish mood came upon John. 'I don't see why we shouldn't make it in some wise official. We're on consecrated ground, after all. Here.' He caught up Sherlock's fingers in his. 'Before my brother and before heaven, I take thee, Sherlock Holmes, for my spouse. I will love, honour and cherish you, and be your partner in all things, to the utmost of that term, for as long as we both shall live.'

An answering waggishness sparked in Sherlock's eyes. 'Is it not an affront to your dignity to have so plain a wife?'

'A plain wife, but a very handsome husband.'

It was foolishness; yet Sherlock was moved. He gripped John's steady hands with a firmness that spoke of the emotion he found so difficult to convey in words.

'I suppose I should say I do.'

'If you like.' John smiled, though.

'I do, then. I'll be your partner in all things, to the utmost of that term. I will love, honour and cherish you, for as long as we both shall live. And if that vow is not good enough for the laws of man, it's good enough, surely, for God, and it's more than good enough for me.'

'Let us go, then, so that I may kiss you in private.'

*

On returning to Melbourne, they first stopped at a menswear store for fresh collars and cuffs for Sherlock. The tailor, horrified at Sherlock's makeshift hemming, insisted on restitching both coat and trousers while they waited – Sherlock sat in the workroom, wrapped in a dressing gown, sipping tea and quietly deducing for John's entertainment the character and habits of several of the customers beyond the curtain by sound alone. A new ready-made suit and a change of underthings were added to the purchases and sent by messenger to their lodgings. In better dress, they next visited the elaborate Federal Hotel and Coffee Palace on Collins Street to dine.

They didn't intend to attend Mrs Gallagher's supper, but by the time they returned to the guest house, the affair had begun and Mrs Gallagher, meeting them by chance in the hallway, swept them into the parlour with inexorable and oblivious cheer.

George, a vivacious young man with a head of Grecian curls, played the piano with graceful verve while his friend, the famed Robbie, sang with a clear, pure voice. The lads gazed at each other as they performed for the small gathering in a manner that could not be mistaken for friendship alone.

Someone had brought wine – 'From Yering Station,' confided a cheerfully soused fellow of middle age, 'They won a Grand Prix at the Paris Exhibition a few years ago. An Australian wine! Imagine! And I got this crate for a song behind the markets!' He then pressed a finger to his lips, said an exaggerated, 'Sssshhhhh' and tottered off.

The fifteen or so artists, writers and musicians made the most of their private fun, talking art and life and love, eating oysters and little pastries and conspiring to keep from Mrs Gallagher the intelligence that she still had a paintbrush jammed into the bun of her hair. Pippin the ugly pug performed admirably as the policeman shot dead by Ned Kelly, and was duly revived by a sausage. This led to a rousing recital of *The Wild Colonial Boy*, said to have been sung at the siege of Glenrowan during Kelly's last stand.

All the guests sang and some of them danced. John and Sherlock sneaked away while the second verse was ringing through the little parlour.

When scarcely sixteen years of age,
He left his father's home,
And through Australia's sunny shores
A bushranger did roam.
He'd rob the largest squatters,
Their stock he would destroy,
A terror to Australia was
The Wild Colonial Boy.

All alone on the stairs, John slipped his fingers over Sherlock's and he grinned. 'When I was a lad, I wanted nothing more than to be a bushranger. It seemed an exciting life.' He squeezed Sherlock's hand. 'Yet I managed to find an exciting life on the right side of the law, in due course.'

Sherlock's eyes held an answering twinkle of amusement. 'On the whole, at least.'

Yet, finally alone in the room, although they kissed, consummation of their graveyard vows didn't immediately follow. Disrobed to nightshirts (both John's) after ensuring the door was closed and latched, they began with tender kisses that grew more insistent, but Sherlock was distracted. He glanced at the bed with a small frown.

'Is everything all right, Sherlock?'

'Yes. Of course.' Sherlock pressed his lips in apology to John's cheek and held him close, but the preoccupation didn't cease and he sighed. 'Even at university when I... first explored these preferences of mine, sharing a bed was a matter of an hour or less. Until yesterday, I have not slept in a bed with anyone since I was an unexpected second child and must share with Mycroft for a time.'

John smiled in sympathetic humour. 'Well I know the rigours of sharing with brothers. Henry used to kick me in the head when he had bad dreams, though he claims I bit him once. Will it salve your concerns if I promise not to bite you?'

'I think I might rather like it if you did.'

So the kissing and explorations with their seeking hands recommenced. Finally in bed, nightshirts discarded for the moment on the covers, they explored one another with mouths, lips, tongues and teeth, while their bodies sought ardent friction against each other, until John spent himself, and then Sherlock, muffling their cries against one another's skin. Afterwards, John succumbed to the urge for affection again, kissing Sherlock's bare shoulders, chest and neck with lavish tenderness. Sherlock delighted in the tickle of his moustache against his skin, but tonight he did not hum.

John found them a clean kerchief to wipe down with. Attired again in nightshirts, they settled in the bed and John, expression wreathed in contentment, fell asleep.

Sherlock was awake for a while, lying on his side and contemplating John's sleeping face. He was thinking of other things too. Henry Watson, and declarations made in the midst of a vast landscape with none but the birds for witnesses.

But what of London? Sherlock thought morosely. *How will your promise hold up once we return to a more crowded, more civilised world?* John no doubt meant all these declarations now, *but what of London?* Sherlock's affair with Victor had not survived outside the sheltering walls of the university, for all the promises made. The disapprobation of the world at large – and Victor's suspicious father in particular – had rendered those promises nothing more than air.

Sherlock refused to let his hopes get beyond the facts as they once did with Victor, and the fact was that John's courage might fail him again.

John slept on, oblivious to Sherlock's scrutiny.

Sherlock could deduce many things about a man, but he couldn't read his mind. He had known for over a decade that John loved and desired him, yet never truly understood the reasons that he didn't act. Understanding them now was a relief. Yet the troubles of the past were difficult to leave behind.

Just as he was finding it difficult, too. Sherlock had put away love and directed his passions towards science, towards the undoubted excitement of solving puzzles. He'd put away physical desire as being a distraction from the mind.

But wasn't love the greatest puzzle, after all? And what had the cocaine been, but a physical distraction for his too-busy brain and too-heavy heart?

And the solution to the greatest puzzle, the provider of the most wonderfully welcome distraction, lay next to him, and he was afraid – *afraid* – that now he had these things, they'd be taken from him. That John, whom he loved, would fail him, as Victor had failed him.

Where days ago had been joy now dwelled uncertainty, and he was doing it to himself, Sherlock knew.

Sherlock swallowed against the irritating doubt and shifted carefully to lay his head on John's chest, to wrap his arm across John's waist, to surround himself with John's warmth and scent.

John shifted, murmured, 'Sherlock,' and cuddled into Sherlock's embrace. He kissed Sherlock's brow and drifted back into sleep.

Sherlock listened to John breathing and then, without meaning to, he also drifted into sleep.

Chapter Fifteen

The two men settled into their cabin on the London-bound steamship *Eastwind* as the ship weighed anchor. Not as handy as the *Lenore Ann* and calling into ports along the way, she'd spend longer on the homeward journey than John had spent coming to Melbourne, but the options had been limited.

Sherlock's belongings took up very little room on one side of John's trunk, though John was inordinately pleased to see them there among his wardrobe and papers. He hadn't yet replaced his medical bag or supplies. He felt unarmed without them, but enquiries proved that this ship at least had a competent doctor on board.

'How will you occupy yourself during the voyage?' John asked, placing the remaining instruments of his profession, wrapped in cloth, into the trunk. 'I have my work organising my case notes, but what will you do with yourself all these weeks? You grew bored enough trapped in Baker Street without a case.'

'I've notes of my own to make – you'll find I have stationery among my effects for the purpose,' Sherlock stated, 'I must consider, too, the best approach to finding Moran, though I have no doubt he'll come to us sooner or later. We'll also discuss how to present our return to London, since your story of my death will be in print by our arrival.'

'Should I wire my editor to withhold the story? We've time....'

'No. Let it be printed. Although Moran knows the truth, we may make use of it yet. I can't deny that I also look forward to disproving the reports of my death with a strategic reappearance.'

'Do not show up unannounced at Baker Street – you'll give Mrs Hudson a nasty turn!' John was caught between humour at Sherlock's puckishness and alarm, for he was known to be a little cavalier in these matters.

'Mrs Hudson is more robust than you give her credit for, but you're right. I'll send Mycroft to her first, to prepare the way.'

'So we shall fill the days with organising my journals. And the nights?'

'Given that we must be careful,' said Sherlock thoughtfully, 'There will be opportunities. For example, we have experiments to conduct.' Sherlock placed his hand on John's knee and flexed his fingers.

'Do we?" John placed his hand over Sherlock's fingers and squeezed.

Sherlock, voice low, said, 'I'd like to catalogue my responses to your moustaches on all parts of my anatomy, and your responses to my hands, about which you have written so often.'

John was all seriousness. 'And naturally we'll have to repeat the experiments under varying conditions within our little cabin.'

'Naturally.'

'My dear fellow,' said John, his grin every bit as roguish as Sherlock's, 'As always, you have thought of everything.'

*

The months at sea sharing a first class cabin were not precisely a hardship, yet neither were they a honeymoon.

Greater care had to be taken in such close proximity with others. The steward would notice if both beds had not been slept in. One mattress hardly held room for two in any case. They shared intimacy, but silence was essential. Footsteps past their door halted activities more than once. Sherlock took himself to the other bed soon after. The stolen moments were joyful, but the necessity for secrecy and discretion coloured the weeks with melancholy.

One night, Sherlock led John belowdecks to the crew quarters where festivities were underway, with music and games. The revelries were much rougher than Mrs Gallagher's soiree, but a more welcome diversion. Sherlock borrowed a fiddle and played tunes from gypsy dances to the Sarasate he'd once hummed underneath the Southern Cross; then, before John could succumb to the emotion stirring in his breast, he played a robust version of *The Wild Colonial Boy*, to make John laugh.

Otherwise, they spent companionable, silent hours together, one or other of them reading or writing in their cabin. For the first time, Sherlock saw the drawings John had made in his notebooks of Sherlock's hands, his eyes, his face. One day, John opened a fresh journal to make notes and found that Sherlock had filled the first ten pages with similar sketches of him.

They promenaded the deck, talking in low voices sometimes of Sherlock's time in exile, or of John's youth in India, England, France and Australia, though they were as likely to exchange views on recent reading, on the behaviour of the passengers and crew, and even Sherlock's capacity to read the weather. The past and the present were their topics of conversation, but not the future, and never their new intimacy.

*

They disembarked in England in early January of 1894, delayed through a storm fifteen days out of port which the *Eastwind* weathered to the cost of a damaged propeller. The sails, stored against such a necessity, were deployed along with rationing and the ship limped into harbour two weeks behind schedule. Sherlock became fractious with the delay and John, as was his habit, even with their transformed relations, suffered the complaints and ill temper stoically. Besides, when Sherlock's better nature reasserted itself, he made up for sharpness with his clever hands, whether on the borrowed fiddle or John's body.

Now, on this frosty January morning, they hastened to find a carriage to take them somewhere warm, neither having sufficient clothing to brave the weather for long. As they saw to the loading of John's trunk on the back of their transport, a message was delivered to them by an apparent fisherman, who Sherlock knew from the shape of his thumb and the state of his trousers to be no fisherman at all.

'Mycroft has news and no doubt a fire.' Sherlock gave the address to the driver, passed the note to John, and sat back in the enclosed carriage, clapping and rubbing his hands together for warmth.

Adair murdered, read John, *Come to the Diogenes immediately.*

In the Strangers Room – the only space at the Diogenes Club where visitors and speech were permitted – a blazing fire and hot coffee revived them as Mycroft explained how Adair had returned to his Park Lane home after an evening playing cards at the Bagatelle Club. Most thought Adair had been in his usual spirits, although those who knew him well had detected a certain agitation: and no wonder. Among his opponents at whist was one Colonel Sebastian Moran, recently returned from abroad. The two men had no opportunity to speak separately, yet the mood between them was definitely aloof.

'Hardly surprising,' said Sherlock, 'What transpired that Moran hasn't been arrested as a suspect?'

Mycroft grinned in delight that his little brother had gone straight to the heart of it. 'We cannot arrest where there is no evidence. Adair was killed in a locked room on the second floor of his home. Soft-nosed expanding revolver bullet. No money stolen. Door locked from the inside.'

'No marks upon the windowsill?'

'Nor footmarks in the garden below, nor on the grass near the road.'

'Of course not. I fancy this will shed light on the matter.' Sherlock drew from his pocket a misshapen lump of metal, which John instantly recognised as the bullet Sherlock had dug from the brickwork after Moran's attempt on their lives on Victoria Parade.

'A soft-nosed revolver bullet, fired from a rifle,' John realised.

'An air gun commissioned from the blind German mechanic, von Herder,' Sherlock said, handing the souvenir over for John to inspect.

'You talked about an air gun before Switzerland.'

'Yes. This weapon has been a favourite of Moran's for some time. This alone is not enough for Moran's arrest, however. Mycroft, may I?' He mimed the need for a coat.

'Of course.'

'And… ah, I shall take these!' Sherlock plucked several books from the shelves – *The Origin of Tree Worship*, *British Birds*, *Catallus* and some others. 'Watson, I must act alone for now. You will remain here?'

'I must return to Kensington to see to my affairs.'

'Ah, Doctor,' interrupted Mycroft, as Sherlock wrapped himself in his brother's voluminous winter coat, took up his hat and set about transforming himself into a crook-backed bookseller, 'I undertook the sale of your practice, as we discussed before your departure. The new owner has not yet taken up residence, but I've taken the liberty of packing what I could of your possessions. I'll join you, to check that everything is to your satisfaction. I'll have my man bring warmer clothes for our short journey.'

John turned to bid Sherlock farewell, but Sherlock had already gone.

*

Doctor Watson, in the company of Mycroft Holmes, returned to his former home to find that old life already packed into crates. The house was silent, devoid of staff and chillingly cold.

This is it. The culmination of my life with Mary and without Sherlock. The house doesn't feel much less empty than when I was living it. Oh Mary. I'm so sorry. You deserved much better than I ever gave you.

Yet he could almost sense her presence here, in this empty house: kind and generous as ever. He could almost hear her voice.

You have found your great friend once more, John. Don't waste your second chance to be happy with him. Love him as I know it's in your heart to love.

John didn't believe in ghosts. He knew it was his memory alone that gave words to her to gift back to him. But he'd wasted enough of his life on doubt and fear and self-recrimination.

He had to do better. By some miracle of fate, he had a chance to do so. He wouldn't allow the shadow of old fear, hovering at his shoulder since their return to London, to cow his intentions.

Neither did it matter that Sherlock had become less and less demonstrative as they approached London, and had now dashed off to complete this case without even a farewell. This great metropolis was not as freeing an environment as the bushlands of Victoria, the streets of Melbourne or even their small steamship cabin. In addition, London was filled with the pain of their older history, as well as many prying eyes. It was strange to be in it again.

Sherlock was right to have let the story of his supposed death be published – a further period of London believing him dead gave them time to settle in to Baker Street, and to each other. They'd need time to adjust, to determine their strategies to remain undetected. Between them, they'd make a life. Until then, he'd be patient.

'I trust that everything meets with your satisfaction, Doctor.'

'Most satisfactory, Mr Holmes. Once I have broached the situation with Mrs Hudson and confirmed that my old rooms remain available, I'll have the necessaries sent to Baker Street and dispose of the rest before the new doctor moves in. February, you say?' John had found a box of clothing and retrieved a warm coat from it, along with a scarf and gloves.

'Or early March. He's moving here from France but prefers to wait until spring. I also took the liberty of visiting Mrs Hudson to let her know that Sherlock was not after all as dead as feared. She expressed a hope that you might both return to your old rooms.'

John donned his own coat and adjusted his scarf. 'She often complained that we were the worst tenants in London.'

'She seems to have missed you, regardless.'

'She has rather Bohemian tendencies of her own,' observed John, 'Though don't tell her I said so.'

'I wouldn't dream of it,' Mycroft assured him warmly. He opened the front door, barring the Doctor's departure with the intrusion of his bulk before leaning to one side slightly, as though to speak privately to the shorter man behind him.

The doorframe beside him burst into fragments of stone.

Mycroft yelped as John dragged him back into the house and slammed the door shut. He leaned his bulk up against the wall, hand pressed to the blood on his jaw while John peered through the curtains at the window, revolver in hand. With a curse reminiscent of his army days, John wrenched the door open and burst onto the pavement to watch as half a dozen men held the struggling assailant prisoner. A police carriage drew up and they bundled him into it. Deprived of his rifle and clothes in disarray, the vicious fellow snarled at John from across the street, before the door closed on him.

'No doubt he's the same ruffian who attempted your life last year,' said Mycroft mildly.

Mycroft, holding a bloodied handkerchief to his face, waved a signal to the men outside. One saluted and the men disappeared with their prisoner as John took Mycroft inside to tend to his injury.

'You did that on purpose,' John accused as he fetched sponges, bandages, alcohol and tweezers from the carefully packed equipment in his old surgery. He washed his hands in carbolic before setting to work.

Mycroft waited until John had swabbed the site before speaking. 'The assassin had to be drawn out, Doctor Watson, and Sherlock would never have forgiven me if I allowed harm to come to *you*.'

Mycroft's tone caused alarm to surge through John's veins. 'You were lucky,' he observed, maintaining a careful bedside manner as he cleaned the scratches on Mycroft's upper neck and jaw. His coat collar had protected him from most of the debris, but his jaw was cut in several places. John pulled out a sliver of stone embedded under the surface of Mycroft's skin. 'His aim was low.'

'Our assassin was expecting *you*, Doctor,' said Mycroft gently.

John had already noted that the shot had been aimed at the standing height of his own forehead.

'Don't be alarmed, Doctor Watson. Do you think I don't know my own brother? Or know when he is happy?'

John felt along Mycroft's skin with his fingertips. Satisfied that no more debris was lodged there, he cleaned the site again, hands steady despite his thundering heart.

'He's reticent I know,' continued Mycroft as reassuringly as John had ever spoken to a frightened patient. 'He was so, even as a child, although the habit was compounded when a friendship soured after university. In truth, I have never seen him so content as he's always been in your society. It's good to see he has a friend in you. So, as I say, if he seems reticent, give him time, Doctor Watson.'

John swabbed the cuts with alcohol and Mycroft gasped at the sting. He waited, silent, while John bundled the bloodied swabs into a receptacle and washed his hands again before applying dressings.

When the doctor was done, he faced Mycroft Holmes with a new calm.

'He and I have spoken of much, since I found him alive in Melbourne. Our return to London has preoccupied us both, I admit. Yet I understand his current reticence, and I gladly grant your brother all the time he needs or wants, Mr Holmes.'

'Oh, Doctor – Mycroft, please.'

John, at ease once more, returned Mycroft's convivial smile. 'Mycroft. And please. Call me John.' Then he nodded towards Mycroft's injury, dressed with a bandage and plaster. 'How is that, now?'

'Much better, thank you John.' Then he shook his head. 'I have never understood how you and Sherlock thrived on this excitement. I look forward to returning to the quiet life.'

'I've had my fill of the quiet life,' said John, eyes sparkling, 'I look forward to the next adventure.'

*

John and Mycroft were reunited with Sherlock at the Diogenes Club, along with an amazed Inspector Bradstreet. The denouement came swiftly after that, in accordance with plans Sherlock had spent weeks devising and the day executing.

Bradstreet and his men followed Sherlock's instructions to lie in disguised wait in Baker Street.

John followed Sherlock on a meandering path from Cavendish Square, which took care that they wouldn't be seen as they darted down alleys and hugged the shadows. Sherlock had refused to divulge the entire plan and John, trusting, simply followed in his steps until he found they were in an upper floor of Camden House, opposite 221B and the window to their old living room. John saw the silhouette of a man moving in the light beyond the curtains.

'How on earth...?' John began, incredulous.

Sherlock quivered with silent laughter. 'It was no mean feat to create it on such short notice, but Monsieur Oscar Meunier, an artisan of no mean skill, was able to alter an existing bust in a few short hours to a sufficient likeness for these purposes.'

'I see he has the shape of your chin and nose down to a nicety,' John observed, voice thrumming with humour.

'Indeed, though the brow is a trifle long.'

'I'd say not, and the shape of the back of the head is exact.'

'You think so?'

'My dear fellow, I have spent many years admiring your profile,' said John in a laughing whisper, 'I could draw it with my eyes closed.' Then he started. 'Good heavens, it moved!'

'Mrs Hudson enthusiastically insisted that she, and not Wiggins as I had initially determined, would take part in this business. She has moved the bust some eight or so times in the last few hours, to support the illusion that I have returned to my former abode. Your Kensington surgery was not the only place under watch. The bust had to be delivered as though it were furniture. I myself conveyed it there in the guise of a delivery man under their very noses. News will have reached Moran, and he'll be in a rush to finish us off. It's as well he wasn't watching Kensington himself, or I might yet owe him a life for Mycroft, or for you.'

They fell silent and were watchful through the dark night until, at last, a sound disturbed them. They withdrew into the deep shadows. Before long, a dark shape had set up at the window, assembling an airgun.

Sherlock wrapped his hand about John's wrist to stay him until a shot was fired across the gap into Baker Street – but then Sherlock leapt like a tiger upon the shooter. The man seized Sherlock by the throat, but John delivered a sharp blow with the butt of his revolver and pinned the dazed assassin to the floor by virtue of a knee at his throat while Sherlock blew his whistle.

Bradstreet and his men soon clattered into the room and were introduced to Sebastian Moran, wanted for the murder of Ronald Adair, not to mention the murders and assaults committed in the colony of Victoria.

*

Sebastian Moran never made it to trial.

Sherlock Holmes suspected that Ronald Adair's father might have found it embarrassing to have the motive for his son's murder – his links to the late Professor Moriarty's gang – made public. Such revelations would surely bring shame and ruin to the rest of the family. Of course, that another old enemy had taken swift revenge was as likely.

Maybe it was just terrible serendipity that on the night of his arrest, Moran fell into an argument with some men in his cell, only to be found dead next morning with bruising to his stomach and lower back. The autopsy showed he'd died of internal bleeding though, said Sherlock on examining his body, someone had certainly muffled Moran's mouth with a large hand to prevent him crying out for aid.

John could not bring himself to mind the lack of courtroom justice. He was too busy supervising the return of his belongings to Baker Street.

Chapter Sixteen

Mrs Hudson was enormously pleased to have her renowned tenants installed in their rooms once more. She even forgave them the shooting out of her window, which had given her such a fright the previous night and showered the carpet in glass.

John expressed concern about the danger she'd been in, but Sherlock dismissed the notion with an absent wave of his fingers. 'Mrs Hudson enjoyed herself immensely. It may have escaped your notice, John, but our landlady is not quite the pillar of respectability she would have us think.'

'She actively welcomes our return as tenants, to begin with,' said John.

'Added to which, I have long suspected that the cook Mrs Hudson employs is not, in fact, her cook.'

John frowned in confusion. '*Not* her cook? But she does cook, Sherlock.'

'I should say, not *only* her cook, and is less an employee than a… *friend.*'

John's eyebrows climbed in surprise, but then he became thoughtful. 'May we depend on her discretion, then?'

'We have always so depended, John. In terms of our future – her situation is not as precarious as ours, under the law,' said Sherlock, 'And yet… I believe we may.'

They sat without speaking in their chairs of old on either side of the fire. This was their first night together again in Baker Street. So far they had not even touched their fingers together.

'You haven't changed your mind, then?' blurted John into the silence.

'No.' Sherlock's reply was terse. Almost breathless.

'Oh, thank God!' The words whooshed out of John, fervently thankful. 'But I understand this may not be easy for you. We're back in London. It's easy to be in love and to show it in the wide open spaces with no witnesses; and I'm aware you'd not wish your work to be clouded by sentiment. I *do* know these things, Sherlock. I wouldn't for the world interfere by demanding more than you're comfortable with. I haven't a fraction of your gifts, but the work you do is important, to me also. I…'

'So your own commitment is unchanged?' Sherlock interrupted the anxious flow.

'I pledged myself to you. For better or worse, in fact.'

'True, but that was, as you say, under an open sky with no witnesses but the two of us.'

'You doubt me then?' John couldn't keep the hurt from his tone.

'I…' Sherlock began, then sighed. 'I'm aware of how dangerous this will be, for both of us. You have seen first-hand the consequences if we fail to be discreet. Even here in our rooms, we must exercise caution, regardless of any sympathy we may receive from Mrs Hudson.'

John's anger suddenly dissolved into a wry quirk of the lips. 'I suppose it's fair, since I asked you first, but to reiterate – Sherlock, I haven't changed my mind. I will not falter. I'm painfully aware of my past failures in this, but Sherlock, I swear to you: you are the best and wisest man I have ever known, and I love you down to my *marrow*. If we cannot be open, yet we have our home. It's a shame that even here we must be vigilant, but at any rate it's better than many like us have. We have no need of unseemly trysts in public places. I'd rather live with you in secrecy, or fly with you in disgrace to another country, than try to live without you ever again.'

Sherlock sat forward in his chair, eagerly searching John's expression for doubt, for self-deception.

He found none.

He dared to hope.

'John. If I have been distant-' he began, but John cut him off by taking his hand.

'You know the truth of my heart and I believe I know the truth of yours. The rest of the world can go hang. I will not deny myself or you again.'

Sherlock listened for sounds beyond their door. Then he kissed John's fingers.

'I am not so articulate in matters of the heart,' he said, 'But believe me, John. What I can't easily say, yet I feel it. *To the marrow.*'

'Show me, then,' said John.

Before the fireplace, they rose. John led the way up the stairs to his room, Sherlock following.

And there, in the privacy of John's room, far above the rest of the sleeping household, John and Sherlock stripped one another, kissing each bared portion of skin revealed to the light of each other's eyes. The need for quiet was still on them, yet not for absolute silence, and each breathed his moans into his lover's mouth; each hummed and groaned his pleasure against the other's skin. They touched and caressed each other, sometimes tenderly gentle, sometimes rough with passion. Teeth scraped across sensitive flesh, soothed immediately after with licks and kisses.

Slick with perspiration and desire, slippery too with a scented oil that proved delightfully suitable for these endeavours, their bodies created and revelled in friction that heightened sensation.

Sherlock pressed his body down onto John; he buried his face in John's neck and took note of a dozen things – the scent of soap; the texture of the end of John's moustache against his cheek, and that of his shaven jaw; John's strong arms around Sherlock's shoulders, sturdy hands on his back, John's splayed inner thighs gripped warm and exciting around Sherlock's hips and the texture of the hair on his chest and belly rubbing against his; the intimacy of their hardness and heat rubbing insistently together, the near sob of pleasure in the back of John's throat (or was it his own?); the warm huff of John's panting breath on his temple, and his low voice murmuring, '*Yes, Sherlock, yes, yes. That's it. Oh, love, oh my dear love, yes, yes, Sherlock, Sherlock, Sherlock.*'

Sherlock abandoned himself to the moment, pressing their foreheads together as their bodies moved, so that he could see the unguarded joy in John's eyes – and allowing John to see the same in him.

Spent, they lay panting together, Sherlock in turn murmuring endearments to John while the quaking of their bodies ceased.

It did not cease.

Sherlock found that John was laughing, torso shaking under Sherlock's weight on him.

'John?'

215

John took Sherlock's face in his hands and kissed him soundly, then proceeded to nuzzle his lips and moustache against Sherlock's throat in the way he knew Sherlock loved. Sherlock stretched his neck accordingly, then buried the fingers of one hand in John's hair, trailing the other delicately over John's shoulders.

'Perhaps I shall write this encounter for that green carnation journal as you suggested,' John said, still laughing with sheer happiness, 'What shall I call it? The Case of the Ardent Detective?'

'The Adventure of the Upright Doctor,' suggested Sherlock wickedly, 'Or How I Solved the Problem of the Soldier at Attention.'

John laughed, then wriggled until he'd turned Sherlock to lie back on the mattress and planted a garden of kisses down Sherlock's throat and chest. 'Will you return to your work?'

'Of course.' Sherlock stroked John's shoulders, his back and hips and the rise of his backside, with the hands that John had for so long adored.

'Good. I like mysteries.' John drew back to gaze fondly into Sherlock's eyes. 'Though you're the best one. You are my favourite mystery.'

How is it that you bring me ease when all my life I never had such a thing? Sherlock thought. *Your joy when I let you see how you affect me brings such pleasure to me, and to see your own deep emotion unmasked at last is likewise profound. I'll never get enough of it, nor truly understand it. You are better than cocaine. You give me both stimulation and rest but do not leave me empty. You fill me up, mind, body and soul.*

None of which he could say yet, so instead Sherlock said, 'And you are my favourite adventure.'

The delight in John's smile pulled an answering one from Sherlock, both dissolving then into laughter that was better than words, then further kissing, which at this moment was better than either. Finally, Sherlock began to hum – a jaunty air of Mozart's – while John nuzzled ticklish moustache kisses against his pale skin.

So they spent the long night, though neither thought it long, considering it to be in every way well-spent.

*

The spring heralded its arrival with persistent rain, turning Baker Street into a muddy ruin and leaving the household trapped testily indoors. Since the winter, news of the return of Sherlock Holmes had filtered through Scotland Yard to less official channels, bringing select cases to their door once more – though not generally on such an unpleasant day as this.

Satisfied that the threat of disturbance was minimal, John had decided to spend the morning sitting on Sherlock's bed to catch up on his reading. Several issues of *The Lancet* lay beside him on the bed as he sat propped against the pillows, half-dressed in his trousers and stockings, his vest and his warmest robe. The fire was blazing very nicely.

Sherlock was fiddling with retorts and beakers in the kitchen, but the experiment concluded more quickly and definitively than he'd expected.

'The Addleton case is resolved,' he called out towards his room, 'The son is innocent, but not the daughter.' He made a note in his journal on the results to send to Bradstreet, which could wait another hour. Perhaps the rain would diminish by then.

Several minutes later, he was in his room with a number of older editions of *The Strand Magazine* in one hand, his unlit pipe in the other. John looked up from an article on the use of the numerous toxicological tests in determining the presence in the deceased of morphine for the 1893 Buchanan murder trial. 'If you are coming to bed,' said John, 'I'd rather the pipe did not.'

Sherlock made a great show of sighing resignation to the edict, but he put the pipe aside and stepped up onto the bed, disrupting its patient occupant until he had settled his lanky frame behind him. John rested against Sherlock's chest and resumed reading. Sherlock placed an arm around John's waist, opened one of *The Strand Magazine* issues on the blankets and leafed through its contents.

'John,' he said after a short interval.

'Mmm?'

'I find myself preoccupied with needing to examine the texture of your hair.'

'You know I'm loathe to deny you satisfaction, Sherlock.'

Accordingly, Sherlock rested his cheek on John's head and combed his fingers idly through the strands above John's ears as he read.

'I have hair on my chest too,' John commented after a time, turning a page.

'Why yes, so I recall.' Sherlock nimbly unbuttoned the top of John's vest and dabbled his fingers underneath the cloth.

He stroked John's chest and kissed a smile against John's neck. John rubbed a free hand against Sherlock's knee.

They remained pleasantly engaged this way while they read for half an hour, until Sherlock flipped the magazine closed. John noted it was the issue containing his erroneous account of Sherlock's end at Reichenbach. He pursed his lips.

'That was indeed most poetic, John.'

John refused to rise to the bait, but Sherlock was not seeking an argument. Instead, Sherlock rubbed his cheek against John's hair and pressed a kiss to his head, as he did whenever a reminder of that bleak past came to them. John folded a hand over Sherlock's, still on his chest.

'I've read all the tales you published during my absence,' said Sherlock, more in the tone John had expected: a little wry, a little fond, a little mocking. 'You embellished the cases considerably. I knew you were a romantic at heart, John, but your efforts draw me as an almost magician-like hero.'

'Of course they don't.'

'And you barely give yourself credit for the contributions you yourself made. You highlighted the business of Ballarat and the cooee in that unsavoury affair in Scotland.'

'You knew those things already, Sherlock, and I had failed to understand their significance within the whole.'

'Your comments highlighted the incidents, John. They were crucial to resolving the case in the young man's favour. You did, in any case, report the St Simon's and Helen Stoner affairs accurately enough...'

'The young lady gave me full permission to use her story and the family name. I checked with Mycroft that the resolution could in no way impugn you. Now that I know that he knew of your survival all along, I assume he's confident you'll face no charges on the matter.'

'Yet you omitted to write that you recognised the swamp adder the moment it appeared. You wrote that you saw a speckled band only and that I named the creature.'

John huffed air against his moustache. 'These stories were designed solely to illuminate your great gifts. They were not meant to shine a light on my contributions.'

'You, my dear John, are surely a great conductor of light, then. I am more magnificent in your stories than I ever have been in life.'

'Nonsense,' scoffed John, abashed, 'You have always been magnificent.'

Sherlock dropped his voice to whisper, sultry, in John's ear. 'As are you. This morning, particularly.' He coloured slightly as he said it.

John, far from blushing, grinned widely. 'I was inspired this morning,' he said, 'By my muse.'

A reprise of the morning's activities may have then commenced, except that the bell by their door jingled to alert them that Mrs Hudson was sending someone up to them.

John kissed Sherlock's brow and then, with the ease of long practice, darted into the living room and up the stairs to his own bedroom, so that he could complete his dress.

Sherlock combed his hair to smoothness and resumed his place at his scientific equipment, which was where Inspector Bradstreet found him. The Inspector accepted Sherlock's notes on the Addleton tragedy, then presented his puzzling facts on the case which had brought him through miserable weather this day.

'One moment, Inspector,' said Sherlock, 'I'll certainly require Doctor Watson's assistance.' He opened the door and shouted up the stairs, 'Watson! Wilson the canary-trainer may finally have gone too far! Will you come?'

John came down the stairs buttoning up his waistcoat, for all the world as if it was his first appearance downstairs this spring morning. 'I'm at your service, Holmes,' he declared, 'How may I assist?'

Epilogue

The sweet strains of Sarasate drifted through the Sussex cottage, riding in on the scent of fresh grass, clover and the lavender they had planted in the spring. Last year it had been heather.

Sherlock experimented with the garden from year to year, and John enjoyed the simple pleasures of digging and weeding. He had his own plot of beans, tomatoes and pumpkin. The asparagus was coming along and next year would be ready to harvest.

John's first stop this morning was collection of the mail, which sat in the basket they left by the front door. Horace, the village postman, was very good about popping the fossilised fern – souvenir of a case – on top to keep the wind from interfering with their correspondence.

At the top was a picture postcard from Bill Wiggins' boy, Bobby. A few days ago, Bobby had taken his dear friend and fellow veteran, David MacKee, to London to be fitted with a new prosthetic leg. 'Davy says the new leg's a corker and much easier than the last,' wrote Bobby, 'He says to tell Mr H we shall be home for the honey harvest on Friday, whatever Mr H always says about not needing us.'

John smiled at Bobby's indefatigable cheerfulness, tucked the rest of the envelopes into his cardigan pocket and limped to the kitchen. He eyed his cane in the umbrella stand by the door and decided he could do without it today. The day was warm and his knee was holding up well. Sherlock, he noted through the kitchen window, had already taken most of the breakfast things into the garden. Only the tea remained to prepare. There, the kettle was just reaching the boil. He poured, stirred the leaves and limped outside with the pot.

'Are the bees charmed?'

Sherlock smiled at John over his bow, and promptly began to play a lively version of *The Wild Colonial Boy.*

John laughed. 'Well, I am at any rate.' He placed the teapot on the little table and the envelopes next to it as he eased into his chair. 'Bobby and Davy will be home on Friday.'

'Good. They can help you with the garden while I harvest the honey. Whatever they say about me needing them.'

Sherlock dropped a kiss onto the top of John's head and sat opposite him, sorting the mail by envelope alone. Even John could see the one from the War Office, which made Sherlock scowl. The Great War had ended last November. They had done their part. John had even written about it and other cases for the sake of morale, with his usual adroit obfuscation of the facts. But they were well and truly retired now and nothing would induce Sherlock to even read the letters.

'Ah, Mrs Hudson writes!' exclaimed Sherlock, not opening that envelope either, 'She and her beloved cook Dot are enjoying their Brighton retirement. And this,' he brandished an envelope at John while John poured the tea, 'Is another of your admirers.'

'Writing to correct my errors once more, I suppose.'

'I wouldn't count on it,' said Sherlock, dropping it so that he could concentrate on coating his slice of bread with honey, 'It's been sixteen years since you published that fanciful story of my return, and only two people have ever written to kindly let you know you that you mistook the date of the Adair inquest.'

'Whereas people never tire of writing to tell me of my wandering wounds as though I don't know my own body.' John took a bite of bread and drank his tea moodily, until Sherlock caught his eye, his expression full of mirth.

'I know your body,' said Sherlock, deadpan, 'And I can confirm every scar and sensitive place.'

John brushed a crumb from his moustache. 'You're incorrigible.'

'A trait I have discerned you find devilishly attractive.'

'True.' John tore open the envelope to see what the letter actually contained. 'Another of these college fellows seeking clarification on a contradiction within the stories.'

'They'll never make sense out of it all,' Sherlock asserted, 'I was there and even I am left bewildered by the amalgam of facts, half-truths and downright lies within your stories.'

'Ass,' John admonished him affectionately, 'You helped me invent half of them. Oh, and this one writes earnestly to tell me he defends us against charges of "unnatural love".' John didn't know if he was more annoyed with himself, for the level of devotion with which he'd still somehow managed to imbue the tales, or with the upstart lad who thought he did them a good turn by denying its existence.

'It doesn't matter a whit what anyone else believes,' Sherlock said, snatching the letter from John's fingers and crumpling it up. 'His prudish opinion is irrelevant and will certainly not keep this old man from taking his dearest love by the hand and down to the willow tree by the brook, where we can dally within its shelter until noon.'

'My dear, you are, as always, the best and wisest man I have ever known.'

'Hardly that,' Sherlock laughed, 'But I have a fancy to listen to you attempt to be silent while I do my best to make you shout my name.'

'Heaven bless our willow tree,' said John fervently, and amused too – that dear tree had given them shelter for many such trysts since they had retired to the Downs ten years before.

He didn't truly mind the impertinence of his letter-writer, who had at the same time declared that the Holmes and Watson friendship was a sacrosanct article. John had not been able to keep the love from his stories, and whether those sentiments were perceived as those of a great platonic friendship or of a more romantic and passionate love, was not the upshot very similar? He had written adventures that were also, in the heart and soul of it, a great love story.

And John Watson was content with that.

Acknowledgements

I'm very excited to see *The Adventure of the Colonial Boy* delivered to the world, and I must pause to give thanks to all the people who helped to make it happen.

So thank you, thank you, Wendy, for inviting me to pitch a story to Improbable Press, and to Steve for creating a press for me to pitch to.

Thank you Tim Richards and Wendy C Fries for proofreading and editing and encouragement. Both of you left margin comments that made me laugh, too, which is such a boon during the editing process!

I send my love to the British Library, where I sat for some happy hours researching things like Victorian steamships, canon-era underwear and sundry topics for the British parts of this story. The City of Melbourne library played its part in checking issues of local history, too. Shout-outs to a lot of great non-fiction writers for other research, including Ruth Goodman for 'How to be a Victorian' and Jurgen Thorwald's three volume 'Century of the Detective' for grounding in the history of forensics.

I also want to thank Dr Craig Hilton for his article "John Watson - The Good Doctor?", exploring whether or not Watson was a good doctor, given his times and the limits of 19th century scientific knowledge, which was the starting point of my research and presentation of John Watson's medical knowledge and skills in this book.

Julia Hilton, a nurse and a generous friend, advised me on the appropriate treatment for snakebite in the late 19th century, and read the chapter in question to make sure I wasn't accidentally killing our hero or making John out to be a terrible doctor.

For all the help and research I did, any errors you find are my own. Some of them may be deliberate – that's certainly what I'll claim if you point them out.

Naturally, my thanks also go to all the incarnations of Holmes and Watson we've been given over the years, from William Gillette and Philippe Laudenbach, to Benedict Cumberbatch and Martin Freeman. Some portrayals I liked more than others, but they've all contributed to the legend and the mythology of Holmes and Watson. Special thanks go to Jeremy Brett and David Burke of the Granada TV series, who were the first Holmes and Watson I loved unreservedly, and who led me to the original stories.

And thank you Arthur Conan Doyle for creating Sherlock Holmes and John Watson, and making them so enduring, and so inviting for writers to play with. However you read their relationship, they offer generation after generation fascination, enjoyment, passion and wonder in the dual pleasures of outré puzzles and great friendship.

At this point, I'd also like to thank over 120 years of fans and fandom for the Great Detective and his Boswell – for all the analyses and articles, the compiled lists of untold cases and the theories about the discrepancies in the original stories. Thank you to the modern fandom for its passion, and for the great community of thinkers and creators who come together to celebrate this fictional marriage of heart and mind, that has been so enduring.

I've played a lot with the original stories: with discrepancies in them, but also generally with the idea of John

228

Watson as an unreliable narrator. In doing so, I've referenced a lot of the novels and short stories, sometimes in ways at odds with how they were originally written. For those who like to keep track, the stories I've reference are:

A Study in Scarlet
The Sign of Four
The Boscombe Valley Mystery
The Speckled Band
The Engineer's Thumb

The Noble Bachelor
The Beryl Coronet
The Gloria Scott
The Final Problem
The Empty House
Black Peter

The Golden Pince-Nez
The Sussex Vampire
The Creeping Man
His Last Bow
The Valley of Fear

I'll leave the fun of re-reading them to find both the references and the discrepancies to you, dear reader, because returning to the source is always marvellous fun.

Narrelle M Harris, February 2016

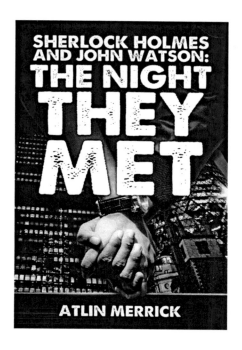

Some things belong together, the one with the other, natural pairs. Sherlock Holmes and John Watson. Holmes and Watson. Sherlock and John. Whether it's in an empty house during the Blitz, a West London strip club in the 70s, or deep in the heart of a Hong Kong computer lab, the meeting of these two legendary men is inevitable. Spanning one hundred and twenty-eight years, here are the stories of that destiny. Of how a detective meets a doctor, of how they change each other in heart and mind. Of how they fall in love.

SOON FROM *IMPROBABLE PRESS*

The Six Secret Loves of Sherlock Holmes

by Atlin Merrick

"Mr. Holmes, have you ever been in love?"

Detective inspector Wanda Payne stood at the head of the Scotland Yard conference table and blinked politely at the perennial burr in her side.

He blinked back at her.

When Sherlock Holmes was seven-years-old he was recognised as a genius.

At nine he was performing chemistry experiments whose formula most university students can neither write nor understand.

When Sherlock was fourteen he learned how little people like the exceptional.

At fifteen he decided he did not care.

Today, at just a bit over forty, the good detective was belatedly learning that exceptional has many sides and some are gifts, like a brain that moves fast as fire when in pursuit of clues, like tongue and fingers, nose and ears that taste touch smell hear the things his eyes do not see.

Yet along with these there's the curse of expecting from exceptional people—yourself and others—exceptional things: Honour, truth, clarity. Not the playground politics of one-upmanship, trickery, or out-right lies.

Detective inspector Wanda Payne, who long ago learned to best rivals with her words because she was too weak to best them any other way, clasped her hands behind her back. She walked slowly around the conference table, behind every one of the twelve Met detectives gathered there and again the DI said, quite courteous, "Have you, Mr. Holmes? Have you ever been in love?"

Sherlock stared at the detective for a long time. So long it could be counted—lub-dub, lub-dub—by a dozen beats of his heart.

And here's a fact: Fascination can be felt. It's a flutter of lashes as gazes shift from a consulting detective, the only one in the world, to a seat across the table from him. It can be tasted in the piquancy of murmurs, smelt in the waft of cologne and perfume as the bold shift in their seats, turning curious gazes toward a quiet man, a familiar man, for where there is Sherlock Holmes, John Watson will always be.

Along with the rest of the men and women in that bare, white room Sherlock looked at that familiar man. Sherlock looked at John Watson, his partner, his biographer, his friend, the love of his life.

Then Sherlock answered the question put to him.

"No, detective inspector Payne, I have not."

SOON FROM *IMPROBABLE PRESS*

All The Difference

by Verity Burns

In a small guesthouse just outside of London, one of the residents is discovered shot dead in his bed on the morning of New Year's Day.

With a finite suspect pool, and under pressure to find a fast resolution, Lestrade resorts to rather drastic measures.

He seeks out a man predictable only in his genius...Sherlock Holmes.

Returning to the scene with his genius in tow, Lestrade is greeted by the news that the case is solved.

Finger prints on the murder weapon lead back to one of the residents, and also prove that he is registered under a false name.

Records show that there is no such person as 'James Wilmington'. The prime suspect's real name is...John Watson.

CPSIA information can be obtained at www.ICGtesting.com
Printed in the USA
BVOW05s1414160316

440585BV00007B/16/P